Early Work

Early Work

Andrew Martin

Farrar, Straus and Giroux

New York

Farrar, Straus and Giroux
175 Varick Street, New York 10014

Library of Congress Cataloging-in-Publication Data
Names: Martin, Andrew, 1985– author.
Title: Early work / Andrew Martin.
Description: First edition. | New York : Farrar, Straus and Giroux, 2018.
Identifiers: LCCN 2017047947 | ISBN 9780374146122 (hardcover)
Subjects: LCSH: Man-woman relationships—Fiction. | Interpersonal
    attraction—Fiction. | Novelists—Fiction.
Classification: LCC PS3613.A77777 E17 2018 | DDC 813/.6—dc23
LC record available at https://lccn.loc.gov/2017047947

Designed by Jonathan D. Lippincott

Our books may be purchased in bulk for promotional, educational,
or business use. Please contact your local bookseller or the Macmillan
Corporate and Premium Sales Department at 1-800-221-7945, extension 5442,
or by e-mail at MacmillanSpecialMarkets@macmillan.com.

www.fsgbooks.com
www.twitter.com/fsgbooks • www.facebook.com/fsgbooks

1   3   5   7   9   10   8   6   4   2

For Laura

Part I

Like most people trying to get by in something like the regular current of American life, I don't act like a total asshole to most people I meet, and am generally regarded as *pretty nice*, mainly because I leave myself vulnerable to hearing out other people's crises and complaints for longer, on average, than would be merely polite. And the fact is, I do tend to like people in practice, even though I've built an airtight case against them in principle. It's a natural response, I guess, to being raised by relatively kind parents who taught me to be polite and decent and to rely on the company and help of others, but to also consider myself smarter and, on some fundamental level, more deserving of complete fulfillment than anyone in the world besides maybe my sisters.

This may be why, when my girlfriend, Julia, asked me to meet her at the house of a recent acquaintance of ours, a New Age–leaning woman named Anna whose family, through what specific brand of plunder I don't know, owned a gigantic house out in horse country, I agreed. Julia would be arriving late from a shift in the ICU and wanted me to be the advance guard. She believed this dinner held the potential for a better-than-usual time, since it brought together a number of people we didn't know very well but had been told we would like. Of course, the "people we would like" often turned out to be amateur poets and holistic healers, but to her eternal credit, this didn't stop Julia from holding out for social transcendence, the nature of which I didn't fully understand. My goals at these things usually extended no further than making at least one moderately clever comment and trying not to spill anything on my shirt.

With the address Julia had given me, I followed my glitchy, ancient GPS to the mechanized gate marking the entrance to Anna's family compound. The architecture ahead was nouveau hunting lodge, polished wood in the kind of low, modernist arrangements I'd encountered at expensive hotels in underdeveloped countries with my parents. I parked in front of something designed to look like a former stable and wandered around the main residence, casing it for an entrance.

As I passed a long window, I saw the profile of a woman staring fixedly into the distance, moving her lips in spirited chatter. Her long dark hair was pulled into a messy upward configuration, held in delicate balance by a pencil, maybe. She stood erect, shoulders squared, but she seemed comfortable, at ease in her formality. She was standing at a kitchen counter, chopping something on a cutting board. This first ghostly observation of Leslie remains significant in my mind, since it was the only time I saw her—ever will see her—without knowing anything about her. In that first long look I couldn't help but notice that she didn't seem to belong in her delicate flowered sundress, that her strong, tanned arms and shoulders were positively bursting out of it. Her bright red lipstick was smeared gooily across her mouth. She looked like a wild creature that had been hastily and not entirely consensually bundled into something approximating midsummer southern chic.

Anna, at the stove, turned to say something to her and caught my eye through the window. Her momentary alarm—this was

during my Allman Brothers phase—quickly turned to enthusiasm, feigned or otherwise, at my arrival. I held up my bottle of
wine and baguette, raised my eyebrows, and mouthed "Door?"
She circled her finger in the air like E.T.: go around, or back
home, whichever. So I continued along the path, drawing a tight
shadow of a smile from the woman at the cutting board, and
eventually arrived at a grand door ornamented with a huge metal
knocker. A long moment later Anna appeared with an orotund
"Oh, *hello*," and I was in.

Anna was magnificently curly headed and just shy of trou-
blingly thin, with a squished cherubic face that seemed to promise PG-13 secrets. She'd grown up in the area and had recently
moved back for somewhat mysterious reasons, possibly involving a now ex-boyfriend's arrest for dealing prescription drugs.
She radiated the kind of positivity that suggested barely repressed
rage.

"You're only the second one here!" she said. "Everyone else
has a *very* loose interpretation of when seven o'clock starts."

"Thanks so much for having me," I said. I took in the wood-
paneled walls, the smudgy, probably authentic impressionist
painting mounted and lit with gallery-grade precision.

"This Bruce Wayne guy sure must be loaded," I said.

"Daddy was a carpenter," she said with a sudden drawl. "But
Granddaddy? He was Dow Chemical." If you had to be rich, it
was best to be self-aware.

"Who else is coming?" I said as we made our way down an
African-mask-lined hallway.

"Well, Lucia *and*, apparently, her new boyfriend, Herman,"
Anna said. "I know I said no couples, but they started dating,
like, between the invite and the actual thing, and I'd invited them
both separately. I mean, what I just said isn't actually true, but
whatever. It's happening. He's fine. And Molly Chang—you know
her? And . . . well, *here* she is. Leslie, Peter."

I hadn't realized from the window how tall she was—nearly six feet, I guessed, to my five eleven plus hair. When she turned from the cutting board, she had a polite nice-to-meet-you grin on her face, but her mouth shaded serious almost immediately, like she'd thought of something important but wasn't sure whether she should say it. My arrival seemed to worry her in some way.

"How's it going?" she said.

She gave me a strong handshake, elbow at a perfectly cocked right angle. My father would have been impressed—he would have asked her what her parents did.

"I'm mostly trying to decide which piece of art to steal," I said.

"Well, it's important to consider both net value and fence-ability," Leslie said. "There's no point in stealing it if you can't sell it. Or so I've read."

"What if I just want something for my house?" I said. "Like, for the love of the art."

"Maybe, instead of stealing my mom's stuff, Pete?" Anna said. "You could pour us some wine and slice up that baguette."

Leslie grinned at me, the full-toothed thing, which, maybe, was the first tentative step into the abyss of the rest of my life, or whatever you want to call it. Love. Leslie went back to the chopping, and I did as I was told.

"So are you . . . visiting Virginia?" I said from the far side of the marble counter.

"Yeah, I live in Austin," she said. "Technically. But really I'm kind of between places. My aunt lives in Louisa, and I figured I could maybe get some work done here. Of course I mostly just lie in the grass wondering whether or not I'm sweating yet, but. It's a start."

"So you work from, uh, home?"

"Yeah, I'm a bum," she said. "Like you, I heard."

I figured she meant writer.

"She's getting paid to write a script," Anna said. "Which is why she can do whatever she wants."

"*Encouraged* is more accurate than paid," Leslie said. "I'm just helping some friends. But fiction's my main, uh, lady."

"That's awesome," I said, which was my default response whenever people told me what they did with their time.

"I've got to figure out whether it is or not," she said. "My brain has almost resolidified now that I've been out of Texas for a few days. Austin? It's like fucking in a sauna, forever."

"So . . . hot," I said.

"Yeah, basically."

The rest of the promised crew arrived in a carpooled crush a few minutes later. I filled wineglasses—pretty much the only thing involving "food" that I could reasonably accomplish—and took stock of the crowd. Lucia was an assistant to an architect by day, a singer in a melancholic musical duo by night. Molly was a hyperactive film buff and the only Asian woman on the local arts scene, in which she held a position of moderate administrative import. Herman was new to me—he appeared to be a mumbling wild card, a mostly skinny man with a gray beard, a beer gut, and mournful eyes. He was of interest only in that he was apparently valued by an interesting woman, which is the most you can say for most men.

I hovered near the bread I'd haphazardly cut and listened to Molly talk at me.

"In a way, it's almost a *good* thing we don't have a quote-unquote indie movie theater anymore," she said. "I mean, that is the most complacent shit in the world. I'd rather watch, you know, Nicolas Cage do like a big-screen reboot of *Nash Bridges* than sit through some happy-sad grown white siblings coming to terms with their gay white parents' death. It's like, I get it, growing up is tough, especially if you're upper-middle class and you're cheating on your spouse and your gay white dad has dementia, but seriously. We can probably survive a few months without that. And if not, I don't know, drive to Richmond."

"I still haven't even been to the drive-in," I said.

"It's pretty great as long as you like the Rock," Molly said. "They literally do not play movies that don't star Dwayne 'the Rock' Johnson. But I don't know, I've been really hot on *performance* movies lately, like concert or sports movies? Performy sports, though, where they have to really *do* the thing. Like have you ever seen *Downhill Racer*? Robert Redford on skis?"

"I think James Salter wrote it," I said.

"Movies don't have writers," she said definitively.

I finished my glass of wine and poured another. I enjoyed Molly's machine-gun approach to conversation, but I knew that it would drive Julia crazy if she ever got here. She didn't feel threatened by women like Molly, she claimed, but she decided quickly that they were superficial and unpleasant. To me, those two qualities on their own weren't much cause for alarm—most of my best *friends* were superficial and unpleasant. A lot of our conversational preferences were based on the gender of the conversant. Julia didn't mind talking to would-be intellectual men, no matter how pretentious they were, as long as they knew things she wanted to find out about, whereas I'd rather chew my hand off than sit at a table being talked down to by some motherfucker working on his dissertation. You only have so much control over your preferences—your real preferences, I mean.

When it was time to eat, I made sure to fall into stride behind Leslie on the way to the dining room, which required a subtle elbow maneuver against Anna to keep her out of my way. It worked; I got a seat immediately to Leslie's right, with Herman on the other side of me. Of course, having never spoken a word to me previously, Herman began talking in my direction the moment we sat down.

"You know, *I'm* a writer," he said, leaning over me to make sure he was addressing Leslie as well. "You read Stephen King?"

"Wait, *you're* Stephen King?" Leslie said.

"No, he lives in Maine," Herman said, unperturbed. "All of his books are about Maine, or most of them at least. I want to be, like, the Stephen King of Maine. I mean, of Virginia."

"So you write horror?" I said.

"Well . . ." He thought this over. "Yeah, I guess you could say that, though you should know that King really doesn't like to be called a horror writer anymore. It's kind of demeaning, like all he's trying to do is *horrify* people, you know? I like to think of both of our work as stories of amazement and fear."

"That's a good genre," Leslie said. "You can fit a lot of stuff in there."

"The Bible, *The Jungle Book*, *The Shining* . . ." I said.

"This one's kind of snarky, huh?" he said.

She put her hand lightly on my shoulder. "I'm getting the sense *this one* fancies himself a real *sophisticated* type."

"It's true," I said. "I only read books without stories."

"Why not skip the words, too?" Leslie said. "Move right along to the cold particularities of life. Herman, Lucia told me you do landscape design? When you're not thrilling and disturbing the reading public?"

"Yeah, you know, it's a living," he said. "I'm starting up a food truck, too. Asian-Mexican fusion."

"*Right on*," Leslie said. She had a deep, clear voice, not rasped by cigarettes, I didn't think, but darker in tone than that of most women I knew. The dim artificial light of the dining room brought out the hard lines and angles of her face and collarbone, like in those wonderful perverted Balthus paintings of girls and cats.

"Y'all can go serve yourselves now if you're ready," Anna said to us, southern again. The other side of the table had been filing out while we talked, so we got up now and filled our bowls from the gumbo-smelling pot on the stove, collecting limp salad greens and servings of a cooked vegetable thing from nearly depleted bowls. I stayed close to Leslie, admiring the back of her neck and the stray strands of dark hair drifting across it.

When everyone was back at the table, Anna explained how she and Leslie met.

"I was in New York, interning at *City Mag*," Anna said. "I helped her get press passes for Fashion Week. Which of course neither of us had *any* fucking clue about."

"I used to work in New York, too," I said. "We probably went to some of the same parties."

"The bad ones?" she said.

"Is there another kind?"

"I'm never going back," Anna said. "Not even to visit."

"I think I read somewhere that Brooklyn's getting cool," Leslie said. "Might want to get in there before it gets expensive."

We moved on to the superhero preferences of Herman's children, and then to Lucia's upcoming show at the town's creepy outdoor "Founder's Day" festival, which was "innovation themed" this year.

"We're supposed to come up with stuff about our performance for the app," she said. "Like I guess they want people to be able to look up things about us *while* we're playing?"

"If you hate enjoying unmediated live music, you'll love this thing!" Leslie said.

"Right, not that I think we deserve anybody's full attention or anything. People will probably like us better if their phone is playing pornographic cartoons or whatever."

"That's what I'm usually looking at on my phone," I said. "Or looking *for*, anyway."

"How does your Julia feel about that?" Leslie said. *My* Julia.

"She's made her peace with it," I said. "We believe in, you know, open borders. Like Obama."

"Have you heard from her?" Anna said. "Do you think she's going to make it out tonight?"

"I haven't," I said, right as I realized that I'd semideliberately left my phone in the kitchen. Like a lot of people, I'd lately been in the habit of trying to go for stretches of time without looking at my phone every ten seconds. Of course a Freudian would say, I don't know, that my phone was my dick, and I left it in the other room because I wanted to have sex with Leslie and didn't want to admit it. Just a guess.

I went to the kitchen and found my phone on the counter. Three texts—"remind me address?" "party still happening?" "where u?"—and two missed calls from Julia. I called her back and she was blessedly unperturbed, or underperturbed, at least. In fact, she said, she'd only just gotten out of the shower and was ready to rock. I wondered if I sounded as guilty as I felt. Probably not, since there was no way for her to know that this particular bout of carelessness was caused by being halfway in love with a clever, unconventionally beautiful woman. It was not, after all, a common occurrence.

I told the table that Julia was on her way, that we had to keep the fun train rolling for her sake. Anna assured me that there was no need to worry—she wanted to have either a game night or a dance party later. I was verbally noncommittal but prayed against a game night. Julia and I were united in our bewilderment at our generation's return to structured activities.

Anna served cobbler and coffee. She really was an excellent host, however many people her family had enslaved and murdered. With the window before Julia's arrival closing, I moved to gather important information with subtle inquiries.

"I'm guessing you've got somebody back in Texas?" I said.

"Is it my dead eyes?" Leslie said. "It's my dead eyes, isn't it."

"Your psychic burden seemed too great for an uncommitted person."

"Well, I'm still *uncommitted*," she said. "Maybe terminally. Which is a not-small part of why I'm up here. It's not really 'fun dinner table chat,' honestly."

"Sorry," I said.

"It's not like it's something wildly lurid or anything. My fiancé and I are having a regular-ass shitty time figuring out what to do. And I'm basically being a huge baby and hiding. I mean, in part because I have all this shit I need to get done. But mostly just because I'm a baby."

"It can't be a bad idea to give yourself a minute to think," I said, which at least had the benefit of being true.

"I know. He's just freaked-out about *me* freaking out. When your fiancée's, like, I need to spend a few months away from you, and she's an emotionally volatile Catholic Armenian, you're kind of forced to reckon with the possibility that things aren't going to turn out very well."

"Well, I hope whatever you want to happen happens," I said. "May the road be always at your feet."

"That's really beautiful," she said. "You must be a really good writer."

When Julia arrived, we'd all decamped to the living room, lounging on the furniture and the floor, neither gaming nor dancing. She entered the room with her arms raised like a boxer, drawing general applause. I got up from my seat on the floor next to Leslie and gave Julia a kiss.

"You made it!" I said.

"Where's my drink?" she said. "I require tequila now."

"Baby, it's not that kind of party."

"Did you hear me say what I required?" she said.

"We probably have some in the liquor cabinet," Anna said.

"Oh no, I was just being silly," Julia said to her. "I mean, I *do* need a drink, though."

"I'll get you a glass of the wine I brought," I said. "It's the tequila of Chiantis."

"Me too?" Leslie said. She held her glass up but remained sitting. I walked back over to her and took it.

"A new friend!" Julia said, with a tiny edge that only I could hear. I filled their glasses in the kitchen and checked my phone. I realized only after I put it back in my pocket that I'd been hoping, irrespective of logic, that I had a text from Leslie.

In the living room, Julia had taken my spot on the floor. She and Leslie already appeared to be deep in chat. I handed over the wine and took a seat on the couch behind them. Of course, I'd forgotten to get another drink for myself.

"Isn't it nice to have someone *do* things for you?" Leslie said. She took a long pull from her glass of wine.

"It's okay," Julia said. "One certainly shouldn't count on it."

"So are you applying for . . . a, what, residency now?" Anna asked Julia.

"Yeah, just about," Julia said. "Reluctantly. Lazily."

"Oh right, you're so lazy," Molly said. "My poor mother would fucking *adopt* you if she could. She *still* asks why I don't apply to med school every time I come home. It's like, Mom, I'm thirty years old and all I want to do is watch movies and apply for grants that will allow me to watch more movies. Focus your attention on the other creature you insisted on imbuing with life."

"For a medical student I'm considered, like, *aggressively* lazy," Julia said. "I read novels instead of participating in masochistic obstacle courses in my free time."

"I admire you for wanting to be a doctor," Leslie said. "I *wish* I wanted to help people."

"Don't worry, it's mostly an ego crusade," Julia said. "As a poet, I'm required to care about myself at least twice as much as I care about anyone else."

"Except for Kiki," I said. Kiki was our dog, a black and tan German shepherd–border collie–something mix, the only being in the world with whom we both had a completely sincere, openhearted relationship.

"*You* love Kiki more than anything else," she said. "I still slightly prefer myself."

I was in love with Julia all over again when she said things like that, and most of the rest of the time, too. We'd had a long five years together, and at that moment we both thought, without quite committing to it, that we'd continue to be together for the long, inevitably more complicated, run. Neither of us quite expected *not* to fuck anyone else for the rest of our lives (and we were in at least theoretical agreement that if one of us *did* happen to do that in the near future it would probably be best not to mention it to the other), but I thought that our relationship might be suited to withstand that, since we were, if we were anything, intellectually compatible. This might be a good place to mention that I had done a terrible job of learning anything about Julia's medical school career outside of the most general understanding of what area of the hospital she was in at any given time.

"Did you get a dog as practice for having a kid?" Molly said.

"Yes, definitely," I said.

"I know you're joking?" Molly said. "But I fucking hate it when people do that."

"All right, guys, two choices," Anna said. "Celebrity, or Cards Against Humanity? Please note that I've got, like, three expansion packs for Cards."

Two hours later we drove home in our separate cars, both of us at least one drink drunker than we should have been for driving. As Celebrity ground on, sowing its promised hilarity, I searched Leslie's face for any sign that she felt remotely similar to me, re: volatile sexual chemistry, but, despite my willingness to read deeply into the smallest hint of such a possibility, I didn't find it. When we hugged goodbye, I made sure not to hold on even a second too long or a degree too tightly.

"*So* good to meet you," she said. "You guys should come over sometime. My aunt's got a good drinking porch. And lots of cups!"

"We'd love that," Julia said, leaning in for her hug.

When Leslie looked back at me, I finally caught a little spark, a frank sizing-up in her brow.

"Write your movie," I said to her.

"Thanks, *Mom*," she said.

In the driveway, Julia gave me a quick kiss and we beeped our respective car locks open. I followed her taillights along back roads, a winding, more scenic route than the one I'd taken to get there. Not that it mattered, since it was so dark.

———·———

Back at the house, once Kiki had thoroughly greeted us—arriving together! after leaving separately!—Julia lay on the beat-to-shit leather couch and I sat in the filthy flowered armchair, reading. Julia was somewhere in the middle of *Patriotic Gore*, a book that I wanted to read in principle but possibly not in practice. I was "waiting until she was done with it," which might be forever. I was in the middle of a very short Argentinean novella, the third tiny book by the author I'd read that month. I was engrossed in a scene in which the protagonist was being mocked by his voluptuous (always voluptuous!) sister when Julia stretched herself out on the couch with a theatrical yawn, then pulled herself into a sitting position.

"I need to go to bed," she said. "Join me for a bit?"

This was a near-nightly ritual. She was working early the next morning, even though it was Saturday, because she was on a six-day rotation. She usually went to bed around ten, which meant she was now up long past her bedtime. I still had a lot more reading and pondering in me. The dynamic this created was not ideal, with her taking on the role of solicitor, me of the interrupted scholar. But it seemed churlish to insist on breaking a pattern that existed for purely practical reasons. My annoyance at being interrupted tended to fade between the living room and the bedroom, and if, once in bed, I thought about the goings-on in the book I'd been reading, well, who *wasn't* guilty of thinking about something else during sex? It was better, probably, than thinking about *someone* else, though that also seemed forgivable. A less forgivable thing would be to *always* think about a *particular* different person, especially if it was a real person whom one saw frequently.

I didn't particularly care if Julia was thinking about someone else, even someone we both knew, unless it was one of three possible men whom I objected to on the basis of their being similar to me but a degree or two more attractive or knowledgeable in some threatening way, and/or if it was one of three possible men with whom Julia had slept directly preceding our relationship. And even if she *were* thinking about one of those six men, my only real objection would be in finding out about it, or if she in some way acted further on this attraction. The idea of her thinking about someone else while we had sex wasn't unexciting to me, in truth, as long as it wasn't about the six particular people I objected to. Sometimes, of course, I imagined her having sex with a vaguely defined amalgamation of men I'd seen in pornography, or specific men I'd seen out in the wild, though usually they lacked faces. So I guess I was getting off on imagining what *she* was imagining while we had sex, which was probably more interesting than what she was actually thinking about, which was in actuality probably just something she'd been reading recently, too, or something someone had said to her at a party, or how long it was until we had to send another rent check.

So I grappled her into position, during which some combination of those thoughts did or didn't appear in her head. She came before I did, and I went on a little longer than either of us would have preferred. Her encouragement became rote, barely distinguishable from incidental sex noises, and I overrode my speculation about the mediocre Argentinean novella with an image of Julia thoroughly engaged by the thrusting of a second abstracted stranger.

And I didn't think about Leslie at all, except to make sure that I wasn't thinking about her.

"Did you like that?" I said.

She nodded with her eyes closed, her peaceful, closemouthed smile portending sleep, or at least signaling the desire to stop communicating.

"I love you," I said. "I'm going to read for a bit."

She nodded again, mouthed "Love you," and curled up toward the wall. I found a pair of dusty boxer shorts that Kiki had dragged under the bed and turned off the light.

In the living room, my book waited on the chair where I'd left it, glowing under the hundred-watt reading lamp that more than vaguely resembled a gallows. I opened the novella and tried to refamiliarize myself with the situation at hand. The sister was negotiating her way across the room, "her sizable breasts setting the pace like the lead dogs on a sled team," to chastise Tomas further for his weakness and cowardice in not standing up to their parents. I couldn't tell if I'd just lost my feeling for the story or if it had truly gotten worse. I read to page 50—"But if your own sense of complicity is damaged, where does that leave the others who have trusted your advice?"—and put the book down.

From where I was sitting, I could see six bookcases, all filled with read and half-read and hoping-to-be-read books. Our small house was packed with stuff, stacked to the ceiling with it, not yet in a pathological way, exactly, but invasive enough to give a sane observer pause. There were books on every surface, books stacked two or three deep in the bookcases and piled horizontally on top of the regular rows, books on the floor, books, I could see in my mind's eye, under the bed, on the bathroom shelves, stacked on top of the unused broken subwoofers in the tiny spare room. Underneath the layer of books on the coffee table was a layer of the country's better magazines that had been piling up for months. There were books and papers and bras and underwear and a recently framed painting on the dining room table, a heavy wood monstrosity that my mother had insisted we take even though it barely fit in the room it occupied, and had now been ruined by our carelessness with coasters and cleaning supplies. There was an orange rolling suitcase on the floor of the living room, still there from Julia's last out-of-town rotation two months earlier, surrounded by clumps of dog hair. There were CDs without cases and record sleeves without records stacked next to a cardboard box filled with records. There was a black cowboy hat and a brown fedora atop the nearest bookshelf, both covered in white dog hair, with a bright red stethoscope, possibly broken, winding around them like a poisonous snake. There were sneakers and boots and dress shoes piled on top of the DVDs at the top of the tallest bookshelf in order to keep them out of the dog's reach.

It was two in the morning but I was still wired. After picking up and putting down two recently published novels, I finally opened my laptop and searched for Leslie's name. It was uncommon enough that her own work filled all of the top entries, and seemed to extend at least onto the next two search pages, and possibly beyond. The "images" row presented three different sizes of a black-and-white picture, clearly used as an author photo at some point, of Leslie looking skeptical in profile, either in an actual photo booth or a setup designed to resemble one, and then two pictures of her at fancy-looking parties, one in which she stood with her arm around a good-looking young man in a tuxedo (her fiancé?), another in which she stood, hunched awkwardly in a designer dress, next to a seated older woman with a regal haircut. (Fashion Week?) I resisted the urge to go directly to Facebook. That wasn't what this was supposed to be about.

The first text result was a piece published on the website of a controversial magazine/media empire, a "story-essay" about a sexual relationship between a college freshman and an unnamed "moderately famous" poet. The sections consisted of graphic recountings of sexual encounters between the student and the poet, with the conceit that the genders of the participants were shuffled in each section, so that in the first, the student was female and the poet male; in the second, both were male; in the third, the student was male, the poet female; the fourth, both

female; and back around again. The "essay" parts consisted of
historical and recent examples of couplings with similar age and
power dynamics, again featuring all possible gender configurations. When I began the piece I assumed, as I was meant to, that
I was reading an autobiographical or thinly veiled account of an
affair the author had actually had, but then found each of the
gender configurations convincing enough that it seemed just as
likely that it was entirely made-up, or based on someone else's
experience, or simply a riff on *Orlando*. This website allowed
comments, and many of them were, basically, "slut." This was
depressing on an obvious sociological level, but I also took the
hostility personally, as if I'd written the piece. I strongly considered, for the first time in my life, type-scrawling a riposte de-
fending Leslie's honor. Instead, I wrote an email to Anna thank-
ing her for dinner and asking for Leslie's email address. Then I
went to bed. I didn't sleep much.

Hey Leslie,

It was so great to meet you the other night! This
town needs more badass writers (especially ones with
no interest in Civil War fan fic) and it's awesome that
you're going to be here for a bit. (I hope, selfishly, for
MORE THAN a bit but realize that "life," whatever that
is, might get in the way.) I read a couple of your pieces
online and really enjoyed them, especially the crazy
original thing for *LEVELUP*. I didn't realize on Friday that
I was meeting the Last Modernist. I'd've probably been
(even) more intimidated.

Anyway this is all winding around to a humble request for you to send me (and Julia!) your SHORT STO-
RIES which the luddite publications you've seen fit to
grace with your word art don't have any interest in dis-

playing for love or money. I can send in return my own nightmarish attempts at prose bending, or in fairer trade, fingers, blood, etc. You name it, I'll send it. Well, not money.

And let's hang out!

Yrs in Christ,

PXC

Hey P,

It was swell seeing you, too. Yr too kind about my stuff, but I'll take it. I'm proud of some of that work, but I do hope the past isn't necessarily prelude, you know? I mean, I guess, that I hope I find some new tricks. Or something.

But, to that end, I'm only sending along one of the other stories I've published, because the other couple are really just too conventional and embarrassing. Obviously I can't stop you or anyone from tracking them down if you/they are so motivated for whatever reason. But I'm not going to aid and abet. Anyway, this is the one I'm still happy(ish) with. It's also the most impossible to find—it was "published" by a friend of mine in what was basically a catalog for an art exhibition that only barely happened (they'll tell you they were "shut down" for being too provocative, but really they were shut down by nobody coming to it and the gallery getting cold feet after a couple of days). It will quickly become obvious to you that I was reading too much Henry James. I need some new influences. Also need to write this dum script. Of course send me anything you want—would rather writing than body parts, but whatever's around'll do.

Give my good regards to Julia, and yeah, let's do some shit. Like . . . next . . . week? Take me drinking someplace I should know about?

Between at least two ferns,

L

I was two years removed from not becoming a doctor of literature. I hadn't understood how PhD programs worked when I applied; I imagined myself writing a long, leisurely essay on a few writers I liked—Evelyn Waugh, Graham Greene, and Muriel Spark?—while cranking out an ambitious but messy first novel about a heroically indecisive teenage alcoholic. It would be like an MFA, but I'd actually learn something. With the help of a hyperbolic recommendation letter written by a kind, unscrupulous senior editor at the content aggregator where I worked, I got into Yale. Julia was thrilled for me. She was just finishing the first year of her premed-for-poets master's degree at Columbia, and thought a Metro-North-based relationship sounded "romantic," though this may have mostly been relative to the romance of my windowless room in the shadow of the Empire State Building in an apartment co-occupied by a sullenly priapic Russian law student and his ill-cared-for cat.

I knew I'd made a mistake within a week of starting classes. Were we supposed to *read* these books? Were my fellow students genuine in their stupid ideas about literature? I thought I could have been friends with the professors, but that was not encouraged. New York, which I had complained about for so long, became a beacon, a place I missed terribly whenever I was away and then glutted myself on until I was sick when I came back. You move away from the city and suddenly everyone wants to have *drinks*. Nobody'll hang out unless you leave.

Julia came to visit plenty, of course, but it felt forced, us trying to find things to like about New Haven. There was some okay pizza, and we saw the Hold Steady at Toad's Place. We got mugged. My apartment was huge, filthy, and barely furnished. My mother insisted on helping me buy an expensive bed that proved extremely difficult to get up the stairs and through the door.

In March, Julia was accepted at three medical schools— Pittsburgh, Penn State, and the University of Virginia. Penn State was out—the medical campus was in Hershey, and Julia hated chocolate. We'd heard good things about Pittsburgh but couldn't find them in action when we visited. The dive bar we'd been recommended was empty. The Vietnamese restaurant was terrible. We'd thought it would be kind of like Philadelphia, but instead it was kind of like Cincinnati. She chose Virginia.

At that point, I figured I'd tough out the PhD, make it make sense. But as the reality of being seven hours away from Julia in a city I didn't understand, doing work I didn't like, surrounded by awful people, sank in, the idea of simply giving up and moving to where she was became a lot more appealing. This medical school thing could be turned to my advantage—I was supporting Julia's career! I was leaning in! And then bang, I'd sell a book in the spring of my first year in Virginia and wouldn't have to go back. Novelists don't need PhDs. They don't need shit.

The money part wasn't that complicated. My parents had set aside cash for me to go to law school, which I was obviously incapable of doing, and after a good amount of back-and-forth, the money became mine, nominally for the purpose of buying a house or funding a legitimate offspring someday. Julia, on the

other hand, lived on loans, the total amount of which was so astronomical as to be not worth contemplating. Infinite debt was
easier to handle than the middle range.

So I took a leave from school to "support Julia" and "write
my book," the second of which people took far too literally.
"How's the book going?" my cousins would ask me at the rare
family gatherings at which I deigned to show my face. "Getting
there," I would say, though as anyone who's ever pretended to
be a writer knows, "the book" was really a handy metaphor for
tinkering with hundreds of Word documents that bore a vague
thematic resemblance to each other, but would never cohere
into the, what, saga of ice and fire that they were imagining.
Not that my cousins, or anyone else, would ever read what I did
produce, a few cramped, obscurely published short stories in-
dicting thinly veiled versions of my immediate family. It was still
"How's the book?" with that shadow of a smirk, not because
they knew I was a fraud, but because they thought I was wasting
my time.

In August, our second month in Virginia, we adopted Kiki,
an action that we both knew, without articulating it, would
make it significantly less likely that I'd ever go back to graduate
school. Then, while desultorily browsing Craigslist for jobs and
furniture, I came across a cryptic listing for a composition in-
structor, "hours flexible due to new government health care
requirements." This turned out to be an official posting by the
dean of English at the Community College in Middle Virginia.
When I arrived in my rumpled tweed jacket for what I thought
was an interview, I found myself filling out adjunct employment
forms. I would be teaching three sections, starting in a week.
For which I was, at the time, grateful.

When Julia and I were undergraduates, she had her poetry published in the prestigious student lit mag and won awards I hadn't even known existed. When she started medical school, she began an epic poem, to be written concurrently with her multiyear education in gore. It was to be Whitman by way of Frank Stanford—ecstatic, despairing, bawdy, democratic, bearded, and mostly about medical school. It may well have been all of those things; the fact was, I'd been privy to very little of it, and the parts I had seen made me a little bit worried about her future, more as a person than as a poet. Julia's defining quality, maybe, was her combination of outer normality, even placidity, and a roiling, crazily volatile inner life that expressed itself mainly in her writing.

In the periods when she was most ensconced in the world of her epic poem, usually during the brief lulls in her demanding hospital schedule, she became glassy-eyed, almost Stepfordian, responding to direct questions with vague pleasantries and spending a great deal of time baking in the kitchen while listening to Chopin. This was her way of building back to mental equilibrium, I knew, but it was somewhat unnerving. What *I* should do, she told me once, after snapping out of a weeklong poetry fugue,

was use these periods as a chance to exercise *my own* creativity—
it was an opportunity for us *both* to write or think or *whatever*
we wanted to do, to feel disobliged to deal with each other's quotidian shit.

I did write a little, mostly beginnings and unconnected
scenes, and endings only in the sense that the stories, or whatever they were, did not continue forever. I didn't have anything
resembling an aesthetic philosophy, but as a person, at least, I was
all middle. I woke up feeling the same as I had when I went to
bed. I *wrote* endings; I just knew they were arbitrary and inadequate. What happens at the end of a story? Something changes, or
it doesn't. I like it best when things just stop.

The community college had a partnership with the women's
correctional center in Louisa County. Teaching at the prison was
a coveted gig because you got double-time pay to teach only once
a week, plus incalculable moral credit. I was neither a distin-
guished, nor a senior, faculty member—the only attention I'd
received from the administration was their intervention in a dispute over whether or not I was allowed to park my car in the
faculty parking area. (I was not.) But, in the hallowed tradition
of the Community College in Middle Virginia, all of the usual
prison instructors had been scheduled to teach conflicting classes
against their explicit requests, and the short summer semester
was offered to me.

The first thing my friends asked me when I started teaching there was whether or not it was like a recent television show that took place in a women's prison. I'd only seen two episodes of the show, but based on that, the answer was no, not particularly. There was not a thin blonde protagonist. There were no quirky backstories involving the Russian mob. There were anxious, exhausted women who, usually in the throes of drug addiction and poverty, had done things they were ashamed of. Per official policy, I was not to ask about what they had done, but, through their reading responses and essays and class discussions, I learned about: accidental and intentional infanticide, gang-initiation stabbings, multigenerational drug-distribution hierarchies, macings of ATM customers, disavowed hate crimes. I had a gift for ingratiation but was ill-suited to be teaching such a class. I extended deadlines into infinity; detected cheating and forgave it; allowed ad hominem, probably dangerous insults to fly unchecked. Throughout my own education, I had always disliked the teachers who insisted on being hard-asses for the good of their students. Even if I now understood intellectually what they'd been trying to do, I still held their enforced standards against them. I was guilty of the worst crime in the profession: I wanted, above all, for my students to like me. And they did, I think, because I generally refused to exercise my authority over them.

It helped that they were, for the most part, diligent, certainly more so than the students at the regular community college, who had to be jostled into a discussion of any kind and given elemental pop quizzes to prove they'd done the reading. ("In 'A Rose for Emily,' who is Emily?") The prison students did the reading and asked for more. We discussed a long essay about whether or not Beyoncé was a feminist, rebutted a *London Review of Books* takedown of Obama's strategy in Syria, nearly came to blows over U.S. immigration policy. (Two students had partners who had been deported.) Though I made lesson plans, I tended to abandon them about fifteen minutes into the three-hour classes. I don't pretend this was pedagogically sound. It—what? It felt right? Their energy overwhelmed my meager planning.

One student, Danita, called me out for the positivity offensive. Her writing was rough, and she knew it, but I kept telling her it was going to get better. And I mean, it *was* going to get better. That's the thing about writing.

"You're a poli*ti*cian, man," she said to me once while I was sitting across from her, going over my comments on one of her papers while the rest of the class peer-reviewed loudly around us. Her hair was close-cropped and she was cadaverously thin. Her eyes stayed calm and accusatory.

"What do you mean?" I said.

"You're telling everybody, 'Oh, you'll get better, you can do it, you're smarter than you think.' But I'm *not* smarter than I think. Sandra's not either. That's why she's *in* here for doing dumb *shit*. Some of them, okay, they actually got something going on; they had an *opportunity* to get a little bit educated. Alicia, you know, she's *educated*. But you're telling *everybody* that? That's not fair, man. That's not fair to *us*."

"All I'm saying is that you're improving," I said. "And that I'll reward your effort."

"So, what? As long as I *try* you're just gonna tell me I did good?"

"Your research on this last paper was really strong."

"I just looked up stuff in a *book*, man, that's all."

"Yeah, well, I've had a lot of students who can't get that part right."

"They probably not *locked up*," she muttered. Meaning they probably had better things to do.

I wish I could say the experience made me appreciate the blessings in my life. Instead, I'd lie facedown on the couch when I got home, exhausted and angry and more than a little bit proud of myself for caring so much.

I spent Saturday reading websites while Julia worked. Then we went and saw the latest bad Woody Allen movie, came home, and drank ourselves to sleep. Sunday was Julia's one day off so we lounged in bed until eleven after throwing Kiki in the yard at dawn, getting up only when her barking got so irritating that we had to let her in. Julia made biscuits and eggs while I handled the coffee and read her selections from the Sunday *Times*, Modern Love first, of course, then the especially obnoxious wedding announcements, then a dumb, negative review of a book that we'd both wanted to read. Once the food was ready we retreated into silence, rotating between the front page, arts, the book review, and the magazine, ignoring everything else.

In the middle of the day, Julia went for a long run and I settled in to illegally stream baseball and distractedly skim a book of poetry my sister had insisted I read, going so far as to buy me a hardcover copy for my birthday. It was aphoristic and wisdom heavy, translated from the Italian, with the helpless originals on facing pages. I was impressed that Jackie could derive so much from this stuff, but its barrenness in my eyes inevitably made me wonder whether she was shining it on a bit.

My sisters and I had turned out artistic and useless despite (because of?) our parents' emphasis on the value of hard work. Our father was a corporate lawyer turned Republican fund-raiser, our mother an administrator at the College of New Jersey (though most of our household swag still proudly identified it as Trenton State, its earlier, somehow more accurate nom de guerre). They'd gotten divorced after almost thirty years of marriage—wealthy Republican women were the unforeseen, if quite foreseeable, occupational hazards of Republican fund-raising. My youngest sister had finally reached college age, and pointedly chose to attend the University of Hawaii after three years of the two-house regime. My other sister was at library school in North Carolina. We saw more of each other than we did anybody else in the family, which still wasn't much.

In the ball game I was half watching, the O's were already down 5–0 in the third—I'd check in after an hour. I opened the file that Leslie had sent me. It was the monologue of an eighteen-year-old girl, a high school senior, who is having a furious, quasi-mystical experience in an abandoned car in the woods after smoking weed (possibly laced with something more serious) for the first time. It was scary in its intensity, transcending the famil-iarity of the premise with a deliberately wonky sense of morality. I liked, both in this and in her poet-screwing piece, the sense of continuation, of unbrokenness, even unfinishedness, a rejection, it seemed, of the conservative narrative conventions currently prevailing. There were no realizations of any consequence, no explanations provided by past trauma. It was all thought and sensation. It's impossible to say how I would have felt about it without having met Leslie. But I'm not an easy mark. It was really fucking good. It was, I thought, exactly what I would have writ-ten if I'd had any idea how.

I resisted the urge to write to her immediately with a burst of unconsidered enthusiasm. Instead I went back through her text, inserting comments intermittently. I quibbled about a few things, suggested commas, line edited a couple of awkward constructions. Then I remembered that she'd told me the piece had already been published, and was, thus, finished, rendering my edits unhelpful. Rude, even. So I deleted everything except for the positive marginal comments, resaved the document, and slammed my laptop shut. Then I herded Kiki, who was leaping all over the furniture with excitement, out to the car for a hike on the trails around Monticello.

In the parking lot I ran into Molly Chang and a tall, fit-looking man clutching a shaking terrier to his chest.

"Hey, Peter! This is Jill," Molly said to me.

"Gil," said the guy, and shook my hand.

"*I* call him Jill," she said. "Is this your *dog?*"

She reached out to pet Kiki, who cowered away with her ears folded back, her default response to new humans. She crept back to sniff the hesitantly wagging tail of Gil's dog.

"You guys doing the Sunday thing?" I said.

"Yeah, it's like a joint walk of shame. Because we're doing it together. And stoned. We stayed up all night watching Tarkovsky and now it's like, shit, *the world*."

"Yeah, I needed to stop reading the paper," I said. "You know what's a bad place? Syria."

"Have you heard about Texas?" Gil said.

"What happened?"

"That's it. Texas. What a shithole."

"Hey, that's where what's-her-name lives," Molly said. "Show some respect."

"Leslie?" I said.

"No, the abortion lady," Molly said. "I'd vote for her. For whatever."

We walked on the paved path that led to the more rugged

trails where the dogs could go off leash. Kiki nipped at the little dog's heels in encouragement.

"What do you do, Gil?" I said.

"I work for ThinkBright?" he said. "We do design and tech consulting?"

"The Lord's work," I said.

"I'm just looking for tall white money to bring home for Thanksgiving," Molly said. "I need six more months out of you, Jill."

We hit the trees and let the dogs bound ahead of us, the little dog taking three times as many steps to keep up with Kiki, who seemed to have caught the scent of squirrel.

"I was thinking, after that thing at Anna's the other night, that we should start a reading group," Molly said.

"I'm not really into book clubs," I said.

"*Not* a book club," Molly said. "More serious. Where we get, like, deep into *texts* and sort out the big questions. And also get fucked-up. And probably mostly just watch movies. It should be, like, *dangerous*. Physically. *And* intellectually."

"I'm not sure I can picture what you're talking about," I said. "But, I mean, sounds good. Sign me up. Don't invite losers."

"*Please*," she said. "You shouldn't have even let that possibility cross your mind."

"Can I be in it?" Gil said.

"Um, you work for ThinkBright," Molly said. "You can pay for our materials if you want?"

"That's really mean."

I was about to tell her to invite Leslie, but thought better of it. Maybe karma would reward me for not pushing things. The dogs started barking wildly and we jogged up the trail to see what was up. We were just in time to watch the retreating white tails of two deer, heading straight for the highway beyond the woods.

Hey, P,

Thanks so much for all the kindness re: my story. I can see lots of problems with it now, of course, but you're a gent not to point them out. All I want anyway is to know that a few people found it moderately amusing or stimulating or whatever. Low standards = still hard to achieve. It was real nice to have yr nice comments. Send me yr stuff sometime?

Phew.

DRINKS? Drinks.

L

Leslie:

Glad to be of use. I'll send something . . . in the glorious alternate future in which I've learned how to write nice.

Also: drinks. Wednesday? Have you been to the 2:19? Fancy restaurant with a great little bar, pictures of writers on the wall? Julia's working nights all this week I think so it might be just me, if that's not too depressing a thought. If we wait an extra week we can rope her in, too.

Yrs truly,

PXC

Naw, dog, let's get to it. Wednesday. 8?

L

I got stoned before I left the house—three good hits from the newish portable vaporizer. It was a beautiful little invention— you could be mildly high all the time, no smoke, no fire. Julia was working two-to-midnight shifts that week, though only Monday, Wednesday, and Friday, so, yes, I had set it up so that I'd be able to spend time alone with Leslie. But it was still, I thought, or pretended, an innocent craving for chat, companionship, artistic solidarity. I was *interested* in Leslie, in the sense that I wanted to know more about her. I wanted to understand her. I wanted her, more dubiously, to understand *me*.

I got to the bar a few minutes early, which was so rare as to be almost unbelievable. Was the time on my phone wrong? Out front, leaning against the restaurant's brick façade, underneath the flaming torch that was lit at dusk every night by the newest member of the waitstaff, slouched Leslie, smoking a cigarette.

"Shit, I knew I wasn't actually early," I said.

"What?" Leslie said. "No, you're good, I think. I never know how long anything is going to take so I got here, like, half an hour ago for no reason."

"You should've called me," I said. "I was just sitting around waiting for eight."

"It's all good. Did some reading, did some drinking. Met Kate the bartender, who's *thrilled* you're coming."

"I had her for comp my first semester of teaching," I said. "She's a pretty good writer. But a better bartender."

Leslie seemed a little bit drunk already, a little bit frayed around the edges. But I thought that I might be overperceiving because I was pretty high, and this made me feel as if I had the ability to detect even the smallest deviation in a person's customary self-presentation, or, maybe, the ability to see people as they actually were.

"I didn't really want you to catch me smoking," Leslie said. "But then it was like seven fifty-two and I really wanted a cigarette, and I thought maybe if you were a couple minutes late I'd be able to finish it and get back inside before you got here. But these American Spirits burn for like *an hour*, and you'd probably have been able to smell it on me anyway."

"Can I have a drag?" I said.

"Yeah," she said. "*Hell* yeah. You can finish it if you want."

"Nah, just a drag," I said, and took one. "Or two. Man, smoking."

"I'd really quit," she said, taking the cigarette back. "And then the second I got to Virginia I found myself walking into a gas station and buying a pack. Just, like, total autopilot."

"Yeah, I hate when I notice that I'm addicted to things. Like, oh, why do I feel so weird today? Oh right, because I'm drunk and stoned from the alcohol I drank and the pot I smoked."

She cast her eyes over me with a new kind of attention.

"Is that really your situation?" she said.

"Oh, I mean, I'm trying to seem cooler than I am," I said. "But there've been some not-great decisions."

"Believe me, I'm with you. I would even go so far as to say *I've* made some not-great decisions. How's that for taking personal responsibility?"

"On that note," I said.

She took a final nubby drag and ground the butt out on the sidewalk. Inside, I nodded to the girl at the hostess desk whose name I could never remember, then went down the stairs into the bar, a narrow, dimly lit cave of unfinished wood. Kate, resplendent in giant glasses, presided. Two tables were occupied by pairs of people, one by an English PhD couple I sort of knew, the other by two old, rich-looking men. There was a fit guy in a polo shirt drinking alone at the bar, a few seats over from a splayed, face-up paperback of *The Beginning of Spring*. Leslie took the seat behind the book and I sat down next to her.

"*He-ey*, Pete," Kate said. She tossed a coaster down in front of me. "What's happening?"

"Just showing this newbie the *coolest bar in town*," I said.

"Only when I'm here," Kate said. "What you drinking?"

"I'll start with a special. What the heck, we made it to Wednesday."

"Good thinking. You good for now, hon?" she said to Leslie.

"*I* want a special," Leslie said. "Does it go with this beer I have to finish?"

"Oh, it goes with everything," Kate said. "Two specials. I'll have one, too, actually. So that's *three* specials."

Leslie looked, I thought, more fully like herself tonight than the first time I met her. She wore no detectable makeup, a plaid, pearl snap-button shirt, jeans. She had her elbows on the bar, like a shift worker kicking back after a day of manual labor, rather than whatever she really was.

Kate returned from the end of the bar with our drinks.

"Are we putting this down in one or what?" she said. There looked to be nearly three shots' worth of booze in each glass.

"I think this might be more of a sipping occasion," I said. "Cheers."

I touched glasses with Kate and Leslie and took a sip; the other two locked eyes and competitively drained their drinks.

"*Fuck* yeah," Kate said.

"What is that?" Leslie said.

"Mostly tequila and lime juice. There's a couple other things I can't tell you about. 'Cause then it wouldn't be special."

"It's a tough little drink," Leslie said.

"Yeah, it does what it does," Kate said. "You want another one?"

"Careful," I said.

Leslie raised her eyebrow and cocked her head at me like a sea captain.

"I'm always careful," she said, rasping for effect. "Let me finish this beer and then we'll see," she said to Kate.

"So, are you liking Virginia?" I said.

"That's a big question," she said. "You know, like, are you liking *the world*?"

I let that stand without comment.

"It's been kind of a rough few weeks, even if my perfect skin belies it," she continued. "I've spent way too much time sitting around worrying about my, uh, conjugal future. Dark rooms and my computer screen are the same pretty much everywhere."

"I realize that must be hard," I said.

"Every time I think about something besides him—us—I realize I need to be thinking about *that*, and it bums me out all over again."

We were, apparently, getting right to it.

"It's not like you're suddenly going to discover some big coherent answer, though, right?"

"No, but I can't tell if I'm having big revelations or if I'm just spending too much time alone. Maybe it's bad that I'm not sure how much I miss him?"

"How much, like, quantitatively, or at all?"

She shrugged the slightest bit with just her shoulder blades, more like a twitch.

"*At all* is a number, too, right?"

The conversation was making me feel more stoned than I'd thought I was, which made me wonder if maybe she was stoned, too, since that would account for the level of intimacy and abstraction we were working at. But maybe this was just exactly how a regular conversation went.

"I think, respectfully, that you should probably get out of the house more," I said. "It's better to make decisions when your baseline emotion isn't misery."

"Right, that leaves, like, an hour a week."

"Whoa, what are you doing for that hour? Share your secret."

She narrowed her eyes. We were flirting.

"Reading," she said.

She excused herself to use the bathroom and I ordered us each another beer.

"Where's your, uh, *usual* lady, pal?" Kate said as she pulled the tap.

"Working," I said. "Unfortunately."

"*Okay*, Prof," she said. "Just be cool. That's all I'm sayin'."

"I'll not make ye a secret-keeping wench, I swear it."

"Oh, please," she said. "Your secrets are *super* not safe with me."

I tapped vacantly at my phone until Leslie settled back down on the stool next to me.

"Anyway, thanks for listening about my life bullshit. At the end of the day, it is what it is, right?"

"When you come to a fork in the road, eat it," I said.

"Okay, but do *you* like *living in Virginia*?" she said pointedly.

"Is *living in Virginia* lowering or heightening your sense of existential dread?"

"My basic status is medium-happy," I said. "We'll have to move when Julia gets the next thing, so it's not useful to analyze it too much. Do I need to have a position? I'm not running for office. I'm not trying to be the president of selfhood."

"Are you kind of fucked-up?" she said.

"Naw," I said, though I was.

"I'm the littlest bit," she said.

"You wanna get some food? The real menu is crazy expensive, but they have good appetizers."

"No no, I'm straight. Unless Kate decided to drug me."

"You ne-ver kno-ow," Kate said in a singsong voice.

"Okay, but seriously," she said, turning on her stool to face me. "What do you actually care about?"

"People," I said.

"All right, E. M. Forster."

I'd been trying to be sincere, but I'd done it so randomly and inexpertly that it had come across as a continuation of banter, an inability to be serious.

"I care about doing good work," I said.

"That's good. I can get behind that."

We sat in silence for a little bit and I felt a sexual current between us, even if it was mostly coming from me. I felt a sharp urge toward *possession*, something that wasn't usually prominent in my taxonomy of desire, and a quality that didn't factor much into what I thought of as my egalitarian relationship with Julia. Right now, sitting with Leslie, I felt bereft over the fact that she wasn't *mine*, that she was going to go back to the place where she lived and stay there until a mutually agreed-upon date, to take place only after a socially acceptable amount of time had passed. It was devastating. Unacceptable.

"I'm just really glad you're here," I said.

"I think I am, too," she said. "You're probably right about being more in the world. Maybe you and Julia can teach me how to live again or something."

"Only by teaching *ourselves* to live can we something something."

"Hey, don't count yourself out of that election yet."

She tipped her chair, steadying herself by gripping the underside of the bar, and rocked back and forth.

"Is there anywhere to even *dance* in this town?" she said.

"Can you dance to bluegrass?"

"I'll make some friends, and then I'll have everybody over to dance to *Dirty Sprite 2*," she said. "And whoever wants to go to trivia or something can go do that wherever."

"*DS2* is definitely the *Terminator 2* of the *Dirty Sprite* saga. Does *Dirty Sprite 1* even exist?"

"Yeah, I'm pretty into monotonous drug rap right now," she said. "I mean, like everybody. I guess it's the usual racist thing, where white people like it because it takes their worst suspicions about minorities and confirms them in lurid and entertaining ways?"

"Yeah, that's why I like it," I said. "Racist reasons mostly. I'm not *thrilled* about the misogyny, though. In my experience, you don't really want to be the guy bringing up the genius of *Yeezus* in a room full of women. Even if someone loves it she'll probably wonder what your problem with women is."

"Girls are going to wonder that no matter what kind of music you say you like. Because guess what: everyone has a problem with women. Because to men? We're a fucking *problem*."

I wasn't sure exactly where we'd gotten to, but I decided to assume we were on the same page.

"Fuck it," she said suddenly, clomping the barstool back down on all four legs. "You want to walk down this, uh, so-called *mall* and have another drink or something? You busy?"

"Naw, Julia's not home till midnight," I said. "And it's, what? Like practically still daytime."

"Oh, good," she said. "I was worried you were going to be one of those *adults* who, like, checks their watch at ten and is like, 'Well, time to go home and let the dog out, gotta get a good night's sleep for the big day tomorrow!'"

"The dog can go a good long time without us," I said, though in truth I spent most of my waking hours worrying about that. "Can we settle up, Kate?"

"So soon?" she said. I could tell she was miffed that we hadn't included her in more of the conversation. We'd treated the queen of Charlottesville like she was some bartender.

"Leslie needs to see the full range of what our fair town has to offer," I said.

"Oh god, you're going to Malone's?" she said.

"We'll see what catches our fancy."

When Kate delivered the bill, Leslie and I huddled over it shoulder to shoulder. She'd only charged us for one drink each.

"On me," Leslie said. "You can get the next ones."

"Okay," I said. "Make sure to leave a good tip."

"Are you serious? I've *been* a waitress, man. Don't even *start* with that shit."

It was the first real anger I'd seen from her. I made a mental note not to tell her what to do.

Leslie paid and we walked down to the claustrophobic pedestrian mall that represented the apex of culture in our under-imagined city. With all of the college students gone for the summer, things were pretty quiet. The afternoon's warm air lingered, trapped by the brick ground and the corridor of shops. Scattered representatives of the bourgeoisie finished dinner or sipped drinks at outdoor tables. A loose knot of black teenagers flowed around us, one girl blasting that song about Versace from her phone. Homeless bearded white men sat on blankets with their dogs behind cardboard signs reading VETERAN PLEASE HELP and EVERY LITTLE BIT COUNTS. On rare occasions, I followed the example set by my friend Kenny, who used to work at the day shelter, and chatted with the guys about what was going on, asked if they knew about the Haven, gave them a dollar. Usually, like now, I just avoided looking in their eyes and kept walking.

"This isn't so bad," Leslie said. "It's fairly active, I guess, for a Wednesday."

"You know they had to bulldoze an entire black neighborhood to build it," I said pointlessly. We walked past an empty restaurant whose walls seemed to be made entirely of glowing televisions.

We walked in silence until we reached Malone's. We stepped through the scrum of smokers to the inside, where a loud band was playing "Guitars, Cadillacs" on the small stage next to the door. A beat-up middle-aged couple danced expressively two feet in front of the band; the guys at the bar and the people drinking at tables seemed to be ignoring the music entirely. I shouted drink orders at the bartender—two tequila shots and two Pacíficos? Modelos? Fine, two Coronas. We took our shots and leaned against the bar, sipping our beers and watching the band. They played "Mind Your Own Business," then an original song I'd heard many times about chickens getting killed by foxes, then "The Race Is On." Leslie grooved a little bit and bobbed her head, but I wasn't getting the sense that she wanted to dance for real, so I didn't try for it.

When they moved, fairly inexplicably given their earlier selections, into a vaguely down-home version of "Cocaine" by Eric Clapton, I waved Leslie over to the stairs at the back of the room.

"Up here's where the magic really happens," I said. We climbed two narrow, increasingly smoky flights of stairs, until we reached a wooden door with a white piece of printer paper attached to it, across which THE 3RD FLOOR was scrawled in Sharpie. I pushed open the door and we stepped into the only smoking bar left in town, grandfathered in by some obscure ordinance that exempted rooms with pool tables that are at least three stories above the ground or something. This was the premier spot for dudes scrounging together the money for one last beer. There was a guy with unapologetic metal hair and a leather vest playing pool by himself, and a fat, angry-faced couple smoking silently over Budweisers at a table in the back. That was it. There didn't even seem to be a bartender.

"Paradise regained," Leslie said. She lit a cigarette and exhaled happily. "Now if there was only some way to get a drink . . ."

We walked over to the bar and stood there, staring at ourselves in the back mirror, willing someone to materialize and serve us. I wondered if Leslie was studying our joint portrait the way I was, whether she was thinking about how good we looked stoic and drunk together, patiently awaiting the agent of our next, important drink. Leslie reached over and grabbed my hand, then held it gently like we were about to recite the Our Father.

"My face is gigantic," she said, still facing forward.

"Good thing it's so pretty," I said.

She turned to me, unsmiling.

"That was a test, you know."

"And?"

She turned back to the mirror. A moment later we heard stomping on the stairs, then watched a tiny bleached-blonde bartender push the door open with her butt and stagger toward the bar with a giant box in her arms.

"Just a minute, guys," she said raspily. She dropped the box on the bar, then ducked through the service area to the other side.

"What is that?" Leslie said.

"What?" the bartender said. "Oh, napkins. I don't know *why* I thought that was necessary just now. Well, now we got 'em. Whaddya guys need?"

"This seems like the whiskey floor," Leslie said.

The bartender poured us generous drinks and we sipped them at a low circular table with a good view of the pool action, of which there wasn't currently much. Vest guy was down to the eight ball but couldn't get it to drop. As I watched his cue ball carom off the rails, it occurred to me that he might have been failing to sink it on purpose. Leslie lit a cigarette and offered it to me, then went back to smoking her own before I could hand mine back. So now I was smoking a cigarette, with my main concern being that Julia would not be happy if I came home smelling like smoke, even though choosing to sit for even five minutes in the smokiest bar in Virginia would make that inevitable anyway. You lose some, you lose some.

"What are you brooding about?" Leslie said.

"What's your fiancé like?" I said. I didn't think I was thinking about that.

"Ummmm," she said. "Well. Brian. He's very into sustainability and food sourcing and all that. He works for this group called Local Food Hub that's all about trying to get organic and ethically grown food into urban areas. Believe me that in Texas this has *not* been easy. Well, it's not so bad in Austin. But he goes to Dallas and they think he's like, some hippie queer. Which of course is a label he'd happily accept, if it were true, but he's really pretty square—in a good way—considering his interests. I mean, I don't think he's gayer than the average guy of his age and cultural sphere. How gay would you say *you* are?"

"Not especially," I said. "How gay are *you*?"

"I've dated women, like everybody, but I never really embraced it as, like, an *identity*. Which can kind of be an issue, or feelings hurting, when you're with someone who's really committed. The old tourist thing. Which I think is a pretty legit criticism. Because, yeah, my life *has* been a lot easier for not having to actually come out to my parents, you know?"

I became aware that I was rubbing the back of my neck excessively, something I do when I'm anxious or drunk, or, as is often the case, both.

"Everybody's life is difficult in a different way," I said.

"Right, and the very rich have more money than we do. Anyway, Brian . . . he's a really great guy, and I don't mean that in the dismissive, somewhat pejorative way that some people use it. I mean I really *love* his goodness. He's, like, the least obnoxious good person I know. He cares about shit, and he gets it done."

"But does that put pressure on you somehow?" I said.

"I thought about that," she said. She swallowed the rest of her drink, along with a couple of pieces of ice, and coughed. "I think the answer is basically no? He makes me more *aware* of the possibility of decency than I might be otherwise, so I guess that's something. That has to be a good thing, right?"

"As long as it doesn't overwhelm you," I said. "And being kind of fucked-up and amoral is an interesting possibility, too." I finished my drink.

"Brian would say, and maybe me too, that it's more interesting to *resist* being amoral and fucked-up. Because for me, at least, it's very easy to be those things."

She said this very solemnly, and my spacious drunken affection for her tightened to a kind of guilt, and sadness. I didn't even know her yet, really, and I felt like we'd gone through an entire relationship cycle, which meant, probably, that it was mostly in my head.

"Peter," she said, still solemn. "I have had slightly too much to drink and should not drive my car. I don't want to make you drive me the, like, thirty-five minutes both ways. On a scale of one to divorcing your ass, how pissed will Julia be if she comes home to me sleeping on your couch?"

"We're not married," I said, too quickly. "And she's a doctor. She'll applaud our prudence."

"Why does 'prudence' sound so disgusting?" Leslie said. "I guess because it sounds like 'prurient'? Or because of the creepy Beatles song?"

"There's nothing creepy about wanting to hang out with Mia Farrow's sister," I said.

I settled up and sent Julia a quick text: "Our new friend LES-LIE needs to stay over tonight if that's all right. Tooooo much fun. Hope works been OK. Love you."

I was feeling a little tipsy myself, so I took a hit of the vaporizer in the stairwell.

"Wait, I want that!" Leslie said. "You holding out on me, bro?"

"Just didn't want to be a pusherman," I said. I remembered, just barely, not to explain to her how to use it.

We paused on the landing between flights and she took a couple of big pulls. I took one more, too, and we descended past the band and out into the still-warm air.

"Does Julia like me?" Leslie said after a couple of minutes.

"I mean, she only met you the once, right?" I said. "But she definitely thought you were cool."

"I got a really good feeling from her," Leslie said. "She gave the impression of being a really special person."

"For sure," I said.

We arrived back at the 2:19, where my Outback was parked out front. I hit the unlock button on my key and the car didn't chirp like it usually did. But the front door opened when I pulled the handle, and I fell into the driver's seat and buckled my seat belt. Leslie picked up a CD off the passenger's seat and got in next to me.

"I wouldn't have pegged you for a Whitney Houston guy," she said.

"What are you talking about?" I said. I put my key in the ignition but it wouldn't turn.

"The *Bodyguard* soundtrack?" she said, holding the CD case toward me.

"Huh," I said, examining the dustless dashboard, the cup holder unfilled by sticky change and stray pieces of dog food. "You know, this isn't my car."

"Like you're borrowing it?"

"No, no," I said. "We should get out. It's somebody else's car."

"Whoa," she said. "Shit."

We just sat there for a minute contemplating this. Then we got out and walked quickly away. No turning back. I remembered that my car was in the parking lot, and sure enough, it beeped obediently when called on. But even in my own car, I couldn't shake the feeling of dislocation. If you could blithely get in the wrong car, do everything but drive away, what else could you do by mistake? Maybe because I spent so much time failing to write short stories, I thought a lot about the arbitrariness of personality, the shuffled randomness of character. I was a certain way because I'd listened to Sonic Youth when I was fourteen; someone else had heard the siren call of Sublime and taken off in another direction. When you analyze people at either a very wide or a very narrow angle, their actions become predictable, regularized. And maybe beauty's in specificity, in the particularities of character, but probably we're just flattering our curiosity, our desire for gossip without social consequences. What's significant, forget beautiful, about a particular triumph or failure? Or: How could it possibly matter which car you get into?

When I started the car, the middle of "You Ain't Gotta Lie" by Kendrick Lamar, which I'd been listening to on repeat all day, blasted out of the speakers. "You ain't gotta lie to kick it, my nigga, you ain't gotta try so hard . . ." over and over again, a not terribly effective mantra.

"Where are you at with this record?" I said.

"I know I'm wrong," Leslie said. "But I really haven't given it much time."

"It's not going anywhere," I said.

It probably wasn't a great idea for me to be driving, legally speaking, but I felt good, floating but focused, directing the car's movement rather than steering. And I loved the blunted calm radiating from Leslie, the coiled potential. I was bringing her back with me. It didn't matter that nothing could happen between us; it was *better* that way. She would be in our little house, sleeping under the same roof, and she wouldn't leave until the morning. On the less positive side, she'd see what a shithole our house was. Which, I realized abruptly, was the thing that would upset Julia about Leslie coming over, rather than anything about her in particular. It was 11:30; I could do a quick straightening before she got home. But the fundamental bombed-out quality—the mountains of dog hair, the grime on the windowsills, the creeping mold on the coffee table—was unalterable. I would have been very surprised if Leslie gave a shit about the cleanliness of the house, but Julia would say that wasn't the point. *She* cared about how it would look, about what it would say about us, our carelessness as humans. And she was right.

I crept the car onto our sleeping block. There was Kiki in the window, majestically perched in full extension across the top of the couch, tail rotoring furiously. When Leslie stepped out of the passenger door, Kiki let out a howl of betrayal and warning: Stranger! Imposter! I shushed her as we walked up the steps to the house. Inside, Kiki externalized her painful inner struggle, greeting me enthusiastically, then turning and barking at Leslie, then jumping up on me, then cowering away when Leslie tried to pet her.

"You're a little tall for her," I said.

"Aw, she'll get used to it," Leslie said. "She'll realize I *am* a dog." She crouched down to Kiki's eye level and said "*I am a dog*" again in a scary Kanye voice. Kiki barked in her face. I put her in the backyard.

"Sorry the house is such a mess," I said. "I'd say it's not usually like this, but."

"Dude, I am a *filthy* person," Leslie said. "This actually looks pretty good to me. Well, not that."

She pointed out a pile of torn-up paper on the floor, at the center of which was a candy bar, still mostly wrapped. I bent down and picked up the detritus.

"This dog," I said. "She'll destroy a bag but leave behind all the food. Which is good, because she'd probably be dead if she ate all this chocolate."

"Okay, but the thing about that," Leslie said. "Do you actually *know* of any dog that died from eating chocolate? Everyone's so paranoid about it, and I guess I believe them, but I've literally never heard of it actually happening."

"I think people are just really *on* it with their preventative measures," I said. "It's pretty much the only thing I know about dog care. And I've had a dog for two years."

I threw away the remnants of the bag, and the candy bar, too. I didn't need to be eating that shit anyway. I still had no reply from Julia—either she was really busy or she was passive-aggressively disapproving of my choices. Probably both.

"You want a beer?" I called from the kitchen.

"Yes please!" Leslie called back.

I grabbed a couple of the metallic-tasting pilsners and sank down onto the big, busted couch cushion next to Leslie, which tipped her toward me, pressing her leg against mine. She unobtrusively shifted back to where she'd been.

"This is good, man," Leslie said. "I feel like we're going to be real friends, you know?"

"Definitely," I said. "Definitely, definitely."

If this had been a regular pickup, if we were an unattached twosome, this, the moment at which we ran out of things to say to each other, would have been the starter pistol for kissing. Instead, we tongued our beers and stared at the wall.

"So, what are you working on now?" Leslie said.

I sighed, performing my frustration with myself.

"Nothing good," I said. "Killing time that could be better spent helping people, or at least making money."

"Man, you can't worry about that too much. Someone could fucking cure cancer with the time I've spent stoned and thinking about, like, the *ideal character-defining gesture*. I get a little hung up about utility sometimes, but I don't know. What else should we be doing?"

I thought about this, took it seriously. I'd been trying to take people at their word lately.

"Nothing," I said, ambiguous even to myself.

I heard Kiki whining frantically from the backyard, and then the *crack* of her hurling her paws into the screen in the kitchen window. This meant that Julia was home. I let Kiki in the back door so that she wouldn't injure herself or the window. She bounded in, then startled into a low growl when she saw Leslie was on the couch, then jumped up on it anyway, staying as far away from Leslie as she could while still looking out the window at Julia's approach.

"Hello!" Julia called out in her dog voice when she walked in. I stepped over and gave her a peck on the mouth, which she accepted with seeming sanguinity. "And hello, wayward sister!"

she said to Leslie, who stood up and gave her a hug. "I'm glad you decided to stay. The cops around here are real dicks."

"I'm sorry for imposing," Leslie said. "I haven't been social-izing much, and all of a sudden I found myself somewhat, um . . . oversocialized?"

"I suppose that'll happen when you're hanging with my boy," Julia said. "And you? You were spared this abundance of fun?"

"I'm bigger," I said.

"Hmmm," she said. "Remember what happened to Kenny, drunk boy."

Kenny'd gotten a DUI on his way home from a raucous read-ing at our house, after which he wasn't allowed to drive for over a year, a punishment that was prolonged when, after having a Breathalyzer installed in his car for a final probationary period, he blew scotch fumes on a hungover morning in my company, which the car's enhanced intelligence dutifully reported to the law.

"I was *meticulous* regarding my intake," I said. Actually, hav-ing this conversation was making me realize how heavy with booze I was. I sank back into the couch. "How was the hospital?"

"I had to stay a little late because I was sewing up this guy's hand," she said. "But, on the plus side, he's like a concert pro-moter or something? So he gave me free tickets to a show at the Southern."

"You must have done a good job," Leslie said.

"Not really," said Julia. "I think he just liked me. Or was looking for someone to like. Let me change out of my blood-soaked garb."

Her scrubs, I should note, looked pretty clean.

Kiki followed Julia into the bedroom, happy to be freed from the choice between outside and us. *This* would have really been the most interesting time to kiss Leslie: I could have found out very quickly what she was all about. Instead I leaned a little closer to her so that our legs were touching again. This time she didn't move away.

"I can drive you back into town to get your car in the morning," I said.

"Oh, I can walk if you have stuff to do," Leslie said.

"I can drop you on my way to teach. So like ten?"

"Whatever works," she said. "Atcher mercy."

Julia reemerged in a T-shirt from a high school production of *Guys and Dolls*, her contacts replaced by heavy glasses.

"So, are we going to get to meet this fiancé of yours?" Julia said. "Or is he not invited."

I supposed I must have told Julia the story, at least as well as I knew it, and hoped that Leslie didn't care.

"He'll actually be visiting in a few weeks," Leslie said. This was news to me. "You guys should totally meet him. I think he and Peter would be fast friends."

"*I* don't care about local food," I said.

"Yes you do," Julia said. "You pick up vegetables from our CSA every week."

"It's not high on my list of priorities," I said.

"Well, he likes baseball and arrogant French New Wave movies and, fucking, I don't know, Otis Redding, too," Leslie said. "Believe me, you'll have plenty to talk about."

I already wanted to fight him.

"He sounds good to me," Julia said. "We're finally going to go to the art museum in Richmond next weekend if you have any interest."

"That's really sweet of you," Leslie said. "I need to make sure my aunt doesn't have anything planned. She likes to show me off to her friends. I know she wants to take me to a freaking *polo* match one of these weekends."

"Oy vey," I said. "If you like assholes, you'll *love* polo!"

"Some of us do, obviously," said Julia.

Leslie leaned back into the sofa, burrowing backward in pleasure.

"Man, you turn into a real curmudgeon sometimes," she said. "It's *very* funny to watch it happen."

"Polo is awful," I said. "I think that's a fair and nuanced position."

"Just your whole *demeanor*," she said.

"Yeah, he's a mood balloon," Julia said. "The booze helps, until it doesn't."

I finished my beer, feeling I didn't have much of a choice.

"Do *you* need a drink, Julia?" I said.

"*I* need to go to bed," she said. "Aren't you teaching tomorrow?"

"Misfortunately," I said.

"Go get some sheets and a blanket for Leslie so she can sleep," Julia said. "I think there are some clean ones in the bathroom closet."

I got up, my earlier annoyance dissipating in the face of Julia's domestic bully routine, which was mostly employed as an adjunct to sex. I guess she'd figured out a pretty swell Pavlovian fix to my attitude. We did have some sheets in the closet, though they were the kind of flowery hand-me-downs that signal "dead old lady" a little too strongly for my taste. Still, they were a better choice than our more aesthetically pleasing, but dirty, alternatives. I went into the bedroom to get a pillow and lingered for an extra couple of minutes to give Julia and Leslie a chance to talk, if they wanted to. When I went back into the living room, the women were silent, though I didn't know whether they had stopped talking when they heard me coming, or what.

"If you need a toothbrush, we have a bunch of unused ones in the cabinet under the sink," Julia said. She laid the sheet over the couch and pushed one side down under the filthy cushions. "Some psychotic Costco binge with my mother."

"Thanks," Leslie said. "You guys go to bed. I'll set up camp here. Y'all are really too kind."

"Not *too* kind," Julia said. She went to the bathroom to brush her teeth.

"Sleep well," I said. "I think we did a pretty good job tonight."

"Many more to come," Leslie said. She had her back turned to me, examining the bookcase in the corner.

"Those ones are mostly Julia's," I said. "She's more committed to the classics."

Leslie took down the gigantic second volume of *The Man Without Qualities.*

"I've always wanted to own this, but I've never gotten through the first one," she said.

"Maybe if you buy the second one, it'll inspire you to finish the first."

"You're pretty good at justifications for buying books, huh?" she said.

"Or you could, you know, borrow it," I said. "I don't think it's in imminent danger of being read."

She put it back on the shelf.

"I'll find something amidst your treasure piles," she said. "Sleep well."

I tried to detect a trace of smirk, but, honestly, I didn't.

In our room, Julia was in bed under the covers. Kiki sighed melodramatically from her monogrammed dog pillow. I crawled from the foot of the bed up to Julia's knees.

"Thank you for being good with all this," I said.

"You seem very proud of yourself," Julia said.

"Just having fun is all."

"I want some, too," she said.

"I thought you had to sleep."

"Soon. Not yet."

I n the morning, after Julia got up and went to work, I moved
as quietly as I could from the bedroom to the kitchen to make
coffee. But when I glanced around the corner, I saw that Leslie was awake, lying across the length of the couch with a book
held over her face and a sheet covering her body. I watched her
read for a minute, her eyes a model of concentration and tran-
quility, her mouth twitching downward in a slight frown. I
recognized the book, a hardcover anniversary reissue of *Blood
Meridian* that I'd poached from my old job.

"Have you read that?" I said finally.

She didn't startle, simply turned her head slightly to acknowledge me while keeping the book aloft above her head.

"In college," she said. "But last night I thought I'd just read
the Harold Bloom introduction in this one to put me to sleep,
and before I knew it I was terrified, so I just kept reading."

"You didn't stay up all night," I said.

"No, no. I fell asleep, and then woke up like an hour ago and
kept reading."

She went back to her book. Kiki barked ferociously in the
backyard at her dog frenemies across the fence. My rule was that
if she barked ten or more times in a row I had to tell her to stop.

She kept making it to seven or eight, then stopping for a few seconds, then going back to it. I had not asked my neighbors how they felt about this rule.

I made coffee and tried to gauge how hungover I was. It seemed like maybe not particularly? Leslie also seemed pretty unfazed. Julia'd said I stank of booze, and I'm sure she was right, but nevertheless, we'd been greedy and thorough with each other. Neither of us mentioned Leslie's presence a short hallway and a couple of thin walls away, but surely it had served some catalytic purpose.

As I was transferring the ground coffee into the stovetop thing, Leslie padded into the kitchen wearing the same rumpled, smoky clothes as the night before. She examined the front of the refrigerator, the baby announcements, wedding invitations, and scrawled reminders about Kiki's tick medication held up by magnets depicting our musical heroes. The household gods.

"I recognize Hank and Bob, but who's the blind guy again? I know that I know."

"Roy Orbison," I said. "He wasn't blind. His family died in a fire."

"That's horrible," Leslie said.

"He was a sad motherfucker," I said. "'Crying' really messes me up."

"I feel like I can't really hear songs like that as *music* anymore, you know what I mean?" Leslie said. "I mean, I *know* it's good, but they're so familiar they just make me feel depressed."

"It's a problem, for sure."

"I need better writing music," Leslie said. "Or maybe I need to just stop trying to listen to music while I write. Or, probably, I just need to find some other way of living."

"It seems like you're doing fine to me," I said.

"Right, you don't really know me."

"Well," I said. She had a point. "Do you want anything to eat?"

"I'm not really a breakfast person," she said. "Though I kind of wish I was, because breakfast is fucking amazing. Breakfast for dinner? *That's* my thing."

There was a moment's pause, and then she stepped forward abruptly and kissed me hard on the mouth. I put my hand to the side of her face and kissed her back, the taste of our sleep-musted mouths canceling each other out, I hoped. It lasted only a couple of seconds, and then she leaned back against the refrigerator with a hint of a smile.

"Let us never speak of it again," she said.

"Oh yeah?" I said.

"It was just one of those crazy mornings," she said.

I stepped forward and kissed her again, more thoroughly this time. Her mouth tasted like stale milk. I pulled her toward me by her hip. She was so warm, so familiar. She ran her hand through my hair, down the back of my neck. I kissed her ear, her cheek, her collarbone.

"You shouldn't be doing this," she muttered near my ear.

I kneaded her ass through her jeans.

"Fuck, man, it's been too long," she said. "Don't tease me like that."

"Like this?" I said. I unsnapped the top couple of buttons of her shirt and kissed her chest.

"Yeah," she said.

I opened the rest of her shirt and kissed the tops of her breasts, pressed my mouth against the maroon fabric of her bra. I got on my knees, kissed her belly button, her stomach spilling out over the top of her jeans. I unbuttoned her jeans and kissed the zipper. I was trying to remember if there were any condoms in the house; Julia had announced the presence of some when we first moved in, half-jokingly explaining where they were "if things got weird." *I* hadn't touched them . . .

"Hey, hey," Leslie said. She grabbed my collar and when that didn't work, my hair, and yanked me to my feet.

"You're being crazy," she said.

"Yes," I said.

"We're in your kitchen, your and Julia's kitchen. With your fucking *dog* in the back*yard*, man."

"It's not ideal," I said.

I stared her down to see if she'd laugh, or kiss me again, but it wasn't happening.

"No, dude, it's not. It's really not."

"I feel a little bit insane about you right now," I said. "This isn't how I usually am."

"We're having a moment of mass hysteria or something," Leslie said. "Not about liking each other. But I don't think we need to fuck in your kitchen this very second."

What I liked about this statement was the implication that we might need to fuck in my kitchen at a later date.

"It would have been fun," I said.

The coffee had been bubbling away for a while now, scorching. I took it off the burner and poured it into cups.

"I heard you guys last night," Leslie said. She was holding her mug to her still-bare chest, not drinking it.

"I'm not saying there's any problem between me and Julia. I just . . . I feel kind of overwhelmed by you."

"You're very sweet," she said.

"I mean, you kissed me," I said.

"And you confirmed my suspicions."

"So your line on this is that you were conducting some kind of experiment?"

"Look, no," Leslie said. "There's no *scheme*, you know? I'm in a weird place, and I realize I'm way too cavalier about things and I'm sorry."

"We're adults," I said, the universal verbal marker of childish behavior. "This doesn't have to be a big deal."

"What doesn't?"

"I mean, stuff like this can happen and it doesn't have to change the course of our lives."

"I wasn't planning to change anything, bud."

"Can continue to happen, I meant."

She set her coffee cup down on the stove and buttoned her shirt.

"I think we should be friends with intense, unspoken potential," she said. "And if something changes in whatever direction, we can reassess."

"That seems really hard," I said.

"Yeah, well, life is full of challenges. Buck up. You just got some sweet action before ten a.m. I'd say you're having a pretty great day."

"Shit, speaking of which," I said. "I've got to go, like, *now*. Are you ready?"

"All I've got is the clothes I walked in with. Do you mind if I borrow your *Blood Meridian*?"

"As long as I can think about you reading it," I said.

"*That's* dark."

I went to the bathroom and splashed water on my face, ran my wet fingers through my hair in a futile attempt to make my bedhead present as respectably disheveled. I threw on some dirty clothes—no jeans at the prison!—and tried to remember what I needed to bring for class. I racked my brain for what I'd assigned them to read—we'd already done "Notes of a Native Son" and "Consider the Lobster," so it was probably . . . the Rwandan genocide. Happy Thursday.

I put a bowl of water in the backyard for Kiki, who put her head on her paws at the daily disappointment of being abandoned. Then Leslie and I trundled out to the car, the stale day-after air of which finally triggered my latent hangover. As we drove away I realized I'd left the front porch light on, but I wasn't about to go back.

Neither of us said anything. The Kendrick album had rolled into the awful fake Tupac interview at the end. I hit the FM button and we listened to Diane Rehm talk to a CDC doctor about Lyme disease.

"Where's your car?" I said when we got downtown.

"Right behind the wrong Subaru," she said. Look at this: we had a past.

I pulled up next to it, a green Camry or something, with Texas plates and a ticket under the windshield wiper.

"Oy, sorry," I said.

"Worth it," she said.

She unbuckled her seat belt and leaned over the center console. I did everything in my power to keep facing forward, and she kissed me demurely on the cheek with a daughterly smack.

I wound my way slowly out to 64 and then gunned it, late, to the prison.

Julia and I started dating in our third year of college, in a Latin American literature class at Columbia. We had been assigned to the same grad student–led seminar, which consisted of the kind of mind-numbing roundtable "discussions" that, in fairness, made the idiocy of my future PhD cohort's comments sound like the fucking wisdom of Socrates.

I first became aware of Julia when I caught her rolling her eyes across the table during an earnest young man's soliloquy about how *One Hundred Years of Solitude* had awakened his soul to the higher truth of human existence. I loved the book, too, of course, as did she. We weren't *monsters*. But I was grateful to see someone as fed up with condescending piety as I was.

"God, I assumed you *hated* me," she said as we walked down Broadway back toward the main campus.

"Why would you think that?" I said.

"You sit there *glowering* the whole time. And *smirking*."

"That's just my face," I said.

"You should work on your face."

We started sitting together in the lectures, and bullied each other into talking during the seminars by saying things like, "Well, Julia was just saying before class that Fuentes is actually parodying this sense of a national stereotype. Or, no, do I have that right, Julia?" and so on. And whatever I'd said, even if I'd made it up on the spot without having read the book, she would improvise a clever response, because she was brilliant, the smartest person in the class, the smartest person I'd met at school, the smartest person I'd met. She was five foot nothing but looked taller because of her long neck and excellent posture. Under that neck, she was all breasts and hips—there was no room for anything else. She had long, curly blonde hair, colored, I learned later, a few shades lighter than it was naturally, and defiantly puffy cheeks that went from a default rosy pink to bright red when she was even mildly embarrassed or drunk. She sang in an early music group, despite the fact that she was a half-Jewish atheist. She was in it for the tunes.

One day after class, I invited her out for a drink. First I had to work at the school newspaper, where I barely edited the arts section, and she had singing rehearsal, but we agreed to meet at 10:30 and walk to the dark punk bar on Columbus that didn't card. At the appointed time, Julia was leaning against the school's front gate. When I got close I could see she was wearing pajama bottoms and a green sweatshirt advertising "the world's largest open pit mine" under her puffy coat. This was, I guess, the cool new nonverbal way of saying we weren't on a date. It brought me down a little, but it also took the pressure off of things. It could be a practice date.

"I actually haven't been to this place," she said as we walked down Broadway, back the way I'd just come. "I know I should have."

"Apparently it used to be heroin central," I said. "Back when the Upper West Side was all fucked-up. You know, like *The Panic in Needle Park*?"

"Good title," Julia said with an odd twinge of regret. It was a good title despite the sad fact that she'd never heard of it? Julia was visibly dragging her feet, stopping at crosswalks even when no cars were coming. In my peripheral vision, I saw her searching my face whenever I was talking.

"Would you rather . . . *not* do this?" I said finally. We stopped in front of the place that served pizza slices larger than an adult human head.

"What? No!" she said. "I mean, unless you want to switch it up. I'm down for whatever."

"Okay," I said. "You don't seem happy."

"I know," she said. She sighed heavily. "I don't really know what your expectations are. I know I'm probably overthinking it. I mean, I definitely *like* you, you seem like a good guy. I just have *way* too much shit going on."

"Yeah, I'm pretty busy, too," I said. "I'm not really asking for some, you know, *time* commitment."

"No, I know. I just . . . this is so awful, but as we're walking, I'm *timing* how long it's going to take us to get to 103rd and Columbus, and how long it's going to take to walk back, and even if we just have like *one drink* I'm going to go to sleep at one, and I'm supposed to meet my stupid friend Jessie for yoga at like the crack of *dawn* for some reason. Sorry, this is unbelievably rude."

"No, I get it," I said, though I didn't, really. It seemed totally ridiculous. "Do you want to just call it a night?"

"Not if you're going to, like, *hate* me," she said. "Maybe you need to just soothingly convince me to have one drink at a place that's a little bit closer. Tell me it'll do me good to chill out for a few minutes."

"The Abbey doesn't card," I said. "And it's right here. I think a beer'll be good for you."

"Do you really think so?" she said. She sounded, somehow, like she was genuinely asking.

"Definitely," I said.

But when we got to the bar, they *were*, in fact, carding at the

door. We told them we'd forgotten our IDs and paused to see if
we might be granted entry anyway. We were not.

"I've got some whiskey in my room," I said. "Let's buy some
ginger ale. You'll be in bed before . . . before you would have
been."

"*Whiskey* in a *boy's room*?" she said. It was clear from the way
she said it that, despite the ironic topspin, it was not something
she had done with any frequency, if at all. We bought the ginger
ale at the bodega on 110th Street and I signed her in at the front
desk of my dorm. The moment the doors closed on the very slow
elevator, I remembered how disastrously messy—borderline personality disorder messy—my room was. (This was a trend, you
see.) When I opened my door, conditions were dire, but not as
bad as they could have been. Yes, there were clothes and books
everywhere, but I hadn't left out any rotting food covered in cigarette butts, as I had before a previous unfortunate rendezvous.

"So this is the dojo," I said.

"Only a little worse than mine," Julia said. I figured at the
time that she was just being nice, but her assessment turned out
to be accurate. When I visited her room a week later, the mess-
iness was the inverse of mine. The books were on the shelves,
the clothes in the drawers, but there was actively rotting fruit
on two surfaces, with swarms of flies hovering over them, and
something mildly unsavory wafting from the squat garbage can
in the corner.

I took the half-full bottle of Jameson down from the top of
the bookcase. I remembered that I owned only one filthy glass.

"Let me go wash this real quick," I said.

Her eyes were already scanning the books lined up across
the dorm-regulation shelf attached to the desk. Books for school,
books from my mother. Boy shit. Dead people.

I ducked out of the room and knocked on Colin's door down
the hall. He answered in just his boxers, clearly already in bed.

"Hey, can I borrow a glass?" I said.

"What?" he said.

"Like, a cup? I have a guest."

"All I have is that giant one. The stein."

"It'll do, pig."

"Whatever," he said. He picked it up off his desk and handed it to me. "Better be a good guest."

"Very promising!" I said. I hurriedly washed the glasses out in the sink in the small communal lounge, then rushed back down the hall to my room. Julia was sitting on the bed with a book open on her lap.

"What that?" I said.

She held it up so I could see the cover: *The Amazing Adventures of Kavalier & Clay*.

"Eh," I said. It was 2007.

She set the book down on the bed. "Should we have this much-promised drink or what?"

"Yes!" I said. "Sorry there's no ice!" It really was stupid. I poured myself a healthy fifty-fifty split of whiskey and ginger ale, which still filled only the bottom third of Colin's giant glass, but gave Julia more manageable measurements in my more manageable cup. We clunked our drinks together and drank.

"Are you dating that girl from the newspaper?" Julia said, as if that first tiny sip had given her immediate mental license to speak freely. "The one I always see you with at the library?"

The girl in question was Edith, who was the film section editor. We weren't dating, but we had slept together. Edith was a hardcore leftist, the kind of person (I didn't learn that this "kind of person" existed until I went to Columbia) who had grown up singing folk songs about the importance of unions, the kind of person who still gathered for protests against the war in Iraq.

"We're just pals," I said. "She's awesome. I think you'd really like her."

"Does *she* know you're just pals?"

"She'd probably say comrades," I said.

"It's none of my business," Julia said. "You just seem . . . interested. And I guess maybe I'm kind of old-fashioned, or up-tight, or however you want to put it."

"Okay," I said.

"Okay, well, I like you," she said. "I know I'm being a freak about it, but I do. But I also don't want to interrupt whatever you're already involved with, and I can't do the, like, hookup thing."

"I get that. Really. I'm happy to just hang out."

"I think you know that's not what I'm saying. Don't be obtuse."

"Well, what do you want?"

"I don't know, do you want to, like, *go out*? With me? For lack of a better term?"

"I do. That's why I invited you out."

"Well, cool. Good. I guess let's drink this drink, then."

It remained a pretty bad drink, but she didn't seem to mind that much. I want to say that I fell in love with her then, saw her sweatshirt and her big glasses, which kept sliding down her nose, in some beatific new light, but I didn't. I was, at that time, more annoyed than excited by her assertiveness, and mad at her for not looking as good as she did to go to class. What was her point? That I had to consent to love her at her worst, even before we started dating? I couldn't tell if it was the ultimate in self-assurance or just the opposite, a failed attempt at self-sabotage.

She told me about her trip to Turkey the year before, when she'd stayed with her roommate's grandparents during Ramadan. They'd been awoken before dawn to eat huge, elaborate meals before the days of fasting.

"I probably *gained* weight in the end," Julia said.

"I love eating, but I forget to do it sometimes. I'll realize I'm hungry and it's like, oh right, lunch. At five o'clock."

"I guess it beats the treadmill," Julia said.

"God, I fucking hate to exercise. I'm really going to try harder."

"I mean, you're not *fat*. But it is, you know, good for you. And good for burning off stress."

"Do I seem stressed?"

"Yeah. Yes. Big-time."

"Well, all right," I said. "Can I kiss you?"

"I guess that'd be okay. I'm not really drunk yet, though."

We kissed a little bit, her tentatively, me trying to, I don't know, prove something. We got horizontal, which, from above, made her face look flushed and devoid of reason, and I kissed her for a while. When I put my hand on the outside of her sweatshirt, somewhere in the general vicinity of her breasts, she pushed it slowly, graciously, away. So we made out a little bit more and then sat up, both of us with our backs to the wall, facing my desk.

"That was fun," I said, hoping that my attempt to sound earnest would register as actual earnestness, even as it sounded vastly hollow to my ears.

"I want to do more stuff," she said. She scooted to the edge of the bed and reached down to get her drink off the floor. She took a long sip. "I just kind of need to take it slow. But I'm, like, *there*, okay? I'm, I don't know, in the bag. You can count it. I just need to, like, defer."

"There's no rush," I said.

She smiled with her mouth open, letting me see her crooked teeth clearly for the first time. Her face was bright red from the booze and the making out and affection, I hoped.

"Can I sleep over?" she said. "I need to leave at like six in the morning, but wouldn't that be fun, you think?"

You don't say no. We turned off the light and lay under the covers in our clothes, me with my face in her hair, periodically nudging it aside so I could breathe suggestively on the nape of her neck. Of course I pressed my body against her, and she tolerated my hand's hesitant explorations for a while before clamping her thighs together and guiding my hand to rest on her stomach, where it lingered, restfully, until dawn.

On Tuesday, while walking Kiki around the neighborhood, I got a call from my friend Kenny. He was, in a manner predictable to everyone but himself, heading out of town for the week on very short notice, driving up to New Hampshire to see his new girlfriend, Cassandra, and play an impromptu jazz show with some buddies. Was there any chance I could go out to his place a few times while he was gone and feed his chickens, collect the eggs, and check on his recently adopted three-legged kitten, who lived exclusively in the upstairs walk-in closet? Of course, I said. He added that I should take as many eggs from the henhouse and vegetables from the garden as I wanted.

"Those cukes are getting threatening, boy," he said. "I don't want to see none of them big green penises around when I get home." I told him I'd go over as soon as I could.

Kenny lived half an hour outside of town in a broken-down farmhouse on a seventy-five-acre property that he rented cheaply in exchange for basic upkeep on the lawn and house. There was a wood-burning stove, a pond, a couple of shotguns, old books, plus the aforementioned chickens and other rotating animals that Kenny found or adopted. I could take Kiki and spend the day

writing and swimming, pretending to be country but still getting to come home to stable Internet access and takeout. And,
well, I could invite anybody I wanted out there.

That night, Julia and I were expected at Molly Chang's for a
"film screening, literary salon, and strategic dislocation," the
apparent manifestation of her book club idea. We'd been asked
to bring "anything that might help facilitate open minds," so I
assembled a mismatched six-pack and we set off across town.
(We were also supposed to have read *Edie: An American Biography*,
but we didn't, and it was never mentioned.)

Molly shared a house on High Street with three cats and a
roommate, all of whom were in the living room when we arrived. After greeting us unenthusiastically, Molly wandered off
to the kitchen, leaving us with the crew. Wedged next to a large
bald man on the couch was: Leslie. She smiled like a guilty
child when she saw us, in a way that seemed to make it painfully obvious that she had things to feel guilty about. But Julia
embraced her first, without a hint of hesitation or remonstrance,
and I did the same. It seemed, momentarily, as if nothing had
happened, and the familiarity of the scene persuaded me that
maybe nothing *had* happened. Adults were allowed to have
fleeting fits of delusion, periods in which they briefly imagined
their lives different, even took a jittery step toward ruin before
retreating, no? If the mistake falls below the threshold of con-
fession, is it really a mistake? Maybe it could be more accurately
categorized as a learning experience.

"You guys ready for some disembodied enlightenment?"
Leslie said.

"Okay, do you have any idea what we're actually watching
or doing?" Julia said.

"I'm pretty sure Molly's planning to show that Michael Jackson movie that was thrown together after he died," Leslie said.

"Which I remember hearing was actually kind of good. But still. If that's the case I'm going to need to medicate quite a bit first."

"Has Michael's death taught you nothing?" I said.

"Oh, man, you got any propofol? *That's* what would really take this party to another level."

The roommate and the cats already seemed pretty medicated; they rolled their eyes in our direction and shifted their necks slightly to acknowledge us, but nothing more. Molly burst back into the room with a small plateful of muffins.

"Here, newcomers, eat these," she said. "You want them to kick in before the feature. They're really strong. Go nuts. But there's no nuts, in case you were worried. There is gluten, though, because fuck you if you don't eat gluten. Sorry, that reference is, like, already dated."

This perhaps explained the state of the room. The baked goods were gigantic and tasted strongly and unpleasantly of weed, and I didn't really trust Molly not to poison us, so I ate only half of mine. Leslie bit into one, chewed thoughtfully, and swallowed.

"Oh right, I already had one of these," she said. "Oh well."

Julia nibbled the corner of mine and put it back on the plate.

"I really don't like being stoned," she said. "But I don't want to be alone."

We opened our beers and passed the others around. Julia and I settled in on the floor in front of the couch, me just to the right of Leslie's feet, Julia next to me leaning against the sofa's arm. The lights cut out abruptly and Molly took the free seat on the couch beside Leslie, behind the stool with the projector balanced on it. Shortly, the desktop of Molly's laptop—a photograph of a beatifically light-bathed topless woman in pink underwear examining a Polaroid—appeared projected on the wall in front of us, followed by an out-of-focus, nineties-era menu screen for *Andy Warhol: Four Silent Movies*.

"Okay, so this is pretty bootleg, because the fucking United States won't properly issue these for some insane reason," Molly said. "But I thought a little bit of AW might be a good way to get us outside of our individualized comfort zones."

She clicked on *Blow Job* and we watched a grainy, overlit shot of a man done up to look like James Dean, his eyes closed in self-conscious ecstasy. He opened his eyes and looked down occasionally, presumably at whoever was engaged with his dick, then sometimes directly into the camera or maybe into the eyes of the cameraman. It was interesting and boring in equal measure, which was almost certainly the point. After he climaxed—no big thing—he lit a cigarette and leaned back, smoking contentedly. That was the best part, the relaxed little joke. The room was dead silent except for the faint buzzing from the speakers. It wasn't sex at all, really.

When it ended after about ten minutes, somebody—the silent dude, I guess—gave a couple of slow claps.

"Okay, now we're going to watch just a little bit of *Kiss*," Molly said. "It's like an hour long, but we'll just watch the first bunch."

So that came on, long black-and-white shots of people kissing for a few minutes at a time, really going at it, but dispassionately, almost clinically. You couldn't help but start thinking about how strange kissing was, how odd it is to spend so much time with your mouth attached to someone else's. But the alternative was true, too—why *shouldn't* two mouths find each other, being of the same basic shape and texture? What better way for a mouth to understand itself than to explore a different one? I wish I could attribute these observations to the drugs taking hold, but it was unlikely, at least in my case, that that had happened yet. I turned to the sofa, to Leslie, Molly, and the other guy, all presumably at least a little bit ahead of me. The guy was frowning; he seemed to be trying very hard to figure out what was going on, as if there were some kind of twist to be sussed out. Molly looked anxious as always, brushing her hair out of her eyes, checking her phone every few seconds to see how much time had passed. Leslie looked adorably stoned, her eyes wide and attentive, her mouth slightly open in awestruck happiness. She noticed me watching her and ruffled my hair, then placed her big hands delicately back in her lap. I leaned over to Julia.

"Does this make you want to kiss me more, or less?"

"Pretty much never again," she said. "I hope that's okay."

"Maybe just little kisses?" I said.

"Only if you wear some kind of mask," she said. "To disguise your human flesh."

By the time Molly stopped the film, on a still frame of a man with glasses deeply engrossed with an enthusiastic long-haired person of indeterminate gender, I was in deep enough to join the group in a disappointed "Awwww."

"Hey, be good or I'll make you watch *Empire*," Molly said. "You'll be here all night."

She put in the next DVD and stood before us in the bright light of the projector.

"Okay, now what you are about to see is a film about the last months in the life of our greatest performer so far, the incomparable genius Michael Jackson. I bet none of you know this, but this summer marks the sixth anniversary of Michael's death, and that is the real reason I have invited you here: to bear witness to his legacy and, through our collective energy, bring him back to our world for a little while longer. Michael was very important to me when I was a little girl. It seemed like I could be him, because we both had long black hair and loved dancing and animals. I even pretended to myself that he was Chinese, and I was so excited watching the 'Black or White' video when one of the people he morphs into is an Asian woman. I spent a lot of time thinking about what it would be like if Michael morphed into me, or if I could morph into him, and feel what it would be like to be singing for all of these people, and to have women fainting and collapsing and wanting so badly to touch me, like I could heal them. I dreamed about Michael all the time, and I know that no one's going to believe me, but the night before he died I think I dreamed that we were sleeping in my bed together and that he told me he wasn't going to be able to perform his last concerts. And I asked him why, and he just smiled and said, with a little quaver in his beautiful voice, 'There's somewhere I have to go, Molly. Don't be sad.' And when I woke up, I knew I was going to find out he'd died, and I tried not to cry because of what he'd told me. But then everybody in L.A. was driving around playing 'Don't Stop 'Til You Get Enough' and 'Man in the Mirror,' and I couldn't help it, it was just so sad. I think it was okay because I was crying just as much from the joy of everyone being united in their love for Michael, and I knew that would have made him happy because he believed most of all in love. And so I haven't cried about it again since, and I think that's important for me. Okay, let's just watch the movie now."

Somewhere in the middle of this speech, I'd started to feel the vibrating high that I'd been anticipating. The light reflecting off of Molly's face had taken on an astronomical quality, and I imagined her standing under a dome of stars, delivering her eulogy to Michael Jackson on a mountaintop in the open air. Julia put her head in my lap, the weight of her skull pressing into my crotch in a not initially unpleasant way.

"All the crazy make me sleepy," she said quietly as Molly turned the lights off.

I leaned back and bumped against Leslie's leg. She shifted, I shifted, and I was against the couch, though her leg remained, ever so lightly, pressed against my gut. Her legs and feet were bare. I didn't think of myself as particularly susceptible to the charms of feet, and these ones were not, in the Platonic sense, anywhere near perfection. The one I had visual access to was long and unwieldy, but with stubby toes that seemed to have been jammed onto the end as an afterthought. A jagged scar ran across her instep. Her foot was also marked up from some kind of shoe, though I couldn't discern, from the bands and divots, what kind it might have been, or what she could have been doing in it to make that kind of pattern. Maybe this was when I really knew things were going to get difficult: I *loved* that foot. I wanted to *know* about it, ask it questions, understand it. I knew it had a story. And since it belonged to Leslie, it would be a good one. I moved my hand so that my pinky bordered her big toe. I felt, I thought, a shiver of recognition. What did feet feel toward hands, their pretentious, elegant cousins? Envy, longing, and distrust.

The Michael Jackson movie was stranger than I'd imagined it could be. I knew it had been "cobbled together," but I hadn't expected a series of long rehearsal takes, shot in ugly low-contrast digital video, with MJ at center stage, lost in his head, trying out an endless series of half-finished dance moves. It was claustrophobic, like being trapped in someone else's nightmare of isolation and stage fright. During a "Billie Jean" rehearsal, in which Michael imitates a robot skeleton while a wedding band vamps listlessly behind him, I started noticing the way he held his sunglasses to his face when he went into a spin, and then I couldn't stop noticing it. It was a child's self-protective gesture, a way of making life slightly more difficult than necessary in order to maintain petty autonomy. I felt tears in my eyes as the song went on and on, whatever meaning it had ever had lost completely in the band's cheerless, perfunctory performance and the widening gulf between their professionalism and Michael's ravaged stabs at dancing, limping along as if under threat, as if in fear that he would be punished if he stopped moving. The man was so thin that it was hard to believe there was even a person under the clothes. The usual comparisons—scarecrow, puppet—didn't begin to do him justice. There was nothing there.

Like many people my age, like Molly, I'd been deeply in love with this man, and had spent hours hurling myself spastically around the house to his songs, and I'd continued to be a partisan of his music and, what, *brand*, until the music got so boring that it wasn't worth the energy anymore. Whatever bad shit he was into, I probably would have stayed loyal if there'd been worthwhile product. The sadness I felt watching the movie had something to do with a person's art betraying them, of watching a man who has grown bored with the possibilities of his craft attempting to find, somewhere in his past, something worth preserving, and finding nothing. Of course, once he died, the rest of us found what he was looking for almost immediately, those perfect content-free jams that everyone knew but hadn't listened to with real attention for so long, "Wanna Be Startin' Somethin'," "P.Y.T.," "Working Day and Night"—the songs relatively untainted by recent hyperexposure and thus absorbed into the cultural subconscious as influences rather than monoliths. I thought about how beautiful he'd been, in his sparkling suit and microphone, backlit by spinning green disco lights, and I wished we could be watching that.

Instead, the movie went on—a bizarre montage of dance rehearsals for "Smooth Criminal" intercut with old gangster movie footage, a harrowingly bad duet of a post-eighties song with a shrieking gospel singer—and I felt my buzzing body recede from any attempt to analyze or assimilate the images on the screen. It became light, just light. What was very important was the weight of Julia's head in my lap, the slight pressure of Leslie's leg, and my increasingly strong conviction that Leslie was transforming my life into something it had not resembled two weeks earlier. The fact that we'd still only spent a handful of hours in each other's company seemed, in that moment, further evidence that something unique and dangerous was at work, rather than leading me to the more rational conclusion that my feelings were ephemeral, and would pass if left unheeded.

I thought about how much happier I'd be if, sitting at Leslie's feet like I was, I had a collar around my neck attached to a leash in her hand, so that I couldn't get up and walk away. Best would be one of those pit bull collars, so I'd have to choose between listening to her and strangling myself to death. Or, better yet, a shock collar, so that I wouldn't be able to speak, either. Julia could be part of it, too, an adjunct, two for one. Leslie could rule over our household like a benevolent dictator, or not so benevolent, whatever. She could choose whichever of us she wanted for the day's tasks, and, at night, exile whomever she chose to the couch or the floor, or, why not, the disused dog crate in the office. It would be up to her. Thus we would carry on as a household on a precipice, always on the verge of catastrophic power shifts and jealous vendettas, but kept in place through one woman's will.

I looked back at Leslie again and remembered that she was a real person, at this moment a real person with a slack jaw and a line of drool dripping out of the side of her mouth. What had Molly *done* to us? And how long was this fucking movie? Julia, I could tell from the rise and fall of her breath, was deeply asleep. So was the big guy on the couch and, it seemed, all of the cats. Molly caught me looking around.

"Movie," she said abruptly. "I mean . . . what? I'm talking now. Are you tired of the movie?"

Leslie turned her head very slowly.

"No, no," she said faintly.

"I was just scoping," I said. "I'm a scoper."

"He's a good scoper," Leslie said. She mussed my hair more distractedly this time, languidly. Caressed, really. It felt so good.

"Do you believe . . ." Leslie said, then stopped. "Sorry, can we talk? Do you believe, if MJ has any postmortem ability to monitor the living, that he's happy with this DVD?"

"Michael wanted to share his gift with the world," Molly said with self-assurance. "And monetize it. As long as he's sharing, and the designated beneficiaries are being compensated appropriately, I think his spirit is satisfied."

Leslie nodded solemnly.

"I hope, when I'm dead?" Leslie said. "That everybody just cools their shit. I'm not saying that dumb thing where, like, *I just want everybody to have a big party and be happy* or anything. But just, you know, congregate, reflect, move on. If there's any money, give it to my brother. Publish anything you can find from my computer if anybody wants it. Go on daytime TV if I died tragic. *I* don't care, I'll be dead. It's not like it can ruin my reputation any worse than what I'll have already done to it."

"I would like my posthumous legacy to be carefully curated," Molly said. "The past is remembered through deliberate shaping. We forget this at our peril."

She was speaking in a formal monotone that was far removed from her usual revved-up style. In the glow of the projector, it gave her entire person a spooky quality.

"Neither of you is going to die," I said. "I'll make sure."

"Do not make promises that you will be unable to keep," Molly said. Now I was pretty sure that she was purposely talking more and more like a robot, to amuse herself or weird us out, or both.

"He's being sweet," Leslie said. "He wants us to live forever."

"That is a really long time," Molly said.

"Not for a robot," I said.

"Ex-cuse me, are you calling me a robot?" Molly said in the robot voice. "I take offense to be-ing characterized as such when I am a liv-ing and breath-ing hu-man."

"Should we turn this off?" I said, tilting my chin toward the screen. Michael was dancing in a teal T-shirt, tight pink pants, and an oversized trench coat; he looked like a shut-in wandering down to the bodega for nonperishables.

"*Fine*," Molly said, reverting to herself. She rapidly hit a series of buttons on the projector and the room faded to pitch dark, though my eyes perceived ghosted light against the wall for a few more seconds.

"I'm assuming everyone's really stoned," Molly said after what felt like five minutes of empty silence. "My basic goal was to, like, incapacitate a roomful of people."

We were silent for another long moment, contemplating this in the dark.

"I think . . . you succeeded," I said. "Where's, ah, Bojo? Think tight? Brain glow?"

"Oh, Jill," Molly said. She exhaled heavily. "*I* dunno, man. I thought it might be kind of *transgressive* or something to date this super-bourgeois dude, but now I wonder if it might just kind of suck. He's smart and all, but I think he just thinks I'm, like, this weird chick."

"In my experience?" Leslie said. "Those normal-seeming guys can turn out to be *super* fucked-up. Sometimes in a good way? Like, they've repressed all this stuff, and then they meet a groovy lady and suddenly they want to try sucking cock and stuff."

"Huh," Molly said. "I guess that would be interesting. If I had a cock."

"I just mean you never know what those normal people are like. They're mysteries. I was with this one guy for a couple of months in Missoula, and I swear, watching *Game of Thrones*, like, flipped a switch in him. All *types* of sex coming out of this dude."

"But everybody just watches porn now," I said. "I mean, so I've heard."

"I think that's just mostly reinforcing very specific mainstream desires in most cases," Leslie said. "Like, 'You want to get fucked hard, slut?' That kind of thing."

"You might be surprised," I said.

"I'm sure *you're* into weird-ass shit. But I'm talking about the wider public."

"Hey, I'm getting wider every day."

"You're going to make a really great dad," Molly said in her robot voice.

"Is the movie over?" Julia said sleepily. She sat up, her hair sticking up like a porcupine.

"The doctor did it," Leslie said. "That's the punch line."

I spent the next couple of evenings at home with Julia, making arguments to myself about our relationship. We had better taste than our friends. We were unconventional without being wacky. We had a rigorously exploratory sex life.

On Wednesday night we made pizza in the UFO-shaped oven Julia's parents had bought us, the heavy-duty kitchen hardware that reads unmistakably as an enticement to start a wedding registry. That refurbished barn, the pizza oven warned, isn't going to pay for itself.

"What do you want on this one?" she said.

"Is there an option that isn't vegetables?" I said. I was leaning against the fridge while she bent over the counter rolling out dough. I couldn't help but remember what had happened the last time I spent extended time in front of the refrigerator.

"Mushrooms aren't vegetables, technically," Julia said. "They're . . . bottom-feeders?"

"Scavengers, I think," I said.

I poured a couple of servings of mezcal and orange juice over ice, then stood behind Julia and held a glass out in front of her face. I clinked it gently against her teeth and tipped it back.

"Mmph," she said. "Correct."

I put the drink on the shaky spice shelf in front of her and went to the front room to put on a record. What said "domestic bliss with a hint of chaos imminent"? Most of our records. I settled on George and Tammy, *We're Gonna Hold On*. "By a fountain back in Rome . . ." came warbling through the static fuzz.

"Our Bach and Tchaikovsky!" yelled Julia. "Is Haggard and Husky!"

"I guess we pretty much *are* the jet set," I said.

"The jet set that would rather stay home."

Julia and I had been all kinds of places—Thailand, Prague, Cleveland. But it was true that I preferred to do nothing. This was not Julia's favorite aspect of my character. I opened the pod to check the progress of the first pizza and was greeted by a gust of black smoke.

"Lost track of that one," Julia said. She took a sip of her drink, leaving smudgy red fingerprints on it. Luckily we'd taken out the smoke detectors long ago. But the pizza was, unfortunately, on fire.

Julia stood on her tiptoes and grabbed the bag of flour off the top of the refrigerator. She poured a pile of it onto the charred pizza.

"One down!" she said. I picked the pizza up by the edges and released it into the trash can. George and Tammy were singing about crawdads with help from some mischievous guitar licks.

"Hey," I said. "You're cute."

"I'm pretty cute," she conceded. She was wearing a T-shirt illustrated with heavily bandaged zombie fingers dripping blood. "All right, this time we *won't* burn the pizza."

By the time we'd cooked all the dough we were fairly drunk. We sat at the dining room table grinning and pulling the pizzas apart with our hands. I thought, blurrily, *Well, we're dumb and we loved each other.*

At the end of the week, I texted Leslie and asked if she wanted to come out to Kenny's place with me for the afternoon. She was down; she'd been holed up trying to write all week but hadn't gotten shit done. Maybe what she needed was to jump in a pond and look at some chickens. In any case, I said, it wouldn't hurt.

I drove out to her aunt's house to pick her up, even though it was in the other direction from Kenny's. It wasn't like I was busy. Kiki lay across the backseat, staring at a fixed point on the car door, either very content or very carsick. It was too hot out, at least ninety-five degrees, and I was running the air-conditioning with the windows open, because there was no one there to tell me I couldn't.

Leslie's aunt's place was a low-slung, wood-cabin thing a long driveway down from a surprisingly busy road. Leslie was sitting on the front porch steps when I pulled up, reading a paperback with her knees up around her ears. Kiki sprang into action behind me, her tail waving furiously at the sight of an overgrown border collie bounding toward the car. Leslie glanced up, then went back to reading until I was standing over her. Kiki raced up to the other dog and feinted out of the way at the last second, then came around and clung industriously to its back left ankle with her mouth, creating a swirling miasma of dog.

"Ready to rock?" I said.

She looked annoyed to be interrupted.

"Should I bring sunscreen?" she said.

"There's some in the car, if you don't mind baby flavor," I said.

She sneered a little and sprang to her feet.

"You read this?" she said. She displayed the frayed cover of *Soul on Ice*.

"I could never bring myself to do it," I said. "I love Baldwin too much. It would feel like a betrayal."

"Yeah, I'm not sure it's actually that good. It's definitely *cool*, though. That counts for something."

She got in the car and I called Kiki back—she reluctantly heeded my fourth command. Leslie rummaged through the loose CDs and broken cases wedged into the car's center console.

"Oh, listen to this first," I said. I'd planned it so that the demo version of "$1000 Wedding" would come on a few minutes after she got in the car, after enough time had elapsed that it wouldn't seem like I'd planned it. "*This* is the saddest shit ever. Worse than Orbison."

We listened to it in silence, me hearing Gram Parsons's trembling voice go through the whole tragic ordeal for the seven thousandth time, Leslie, I assumed, for the first. I imagined we were sharing a moment of charged, awestruck wonder.

When it ended she said: "A little overwrought, no?"

"Did you hear him?" I said. "'*With all the invitations sent, the young bride passed away*'! Is the situation not *deserving* of some emotion?"

"It's not like it's something that happened and he *had* to report on it. It's all just Parsons co-opting what he imagines to be the pure yokel cornpone heart. I'm not saying it's not pretty.

He's a nice singer. I don't know, for some reason every time I listen to him, I just think *Oooh-kay, Gram, thank you, you are a very sad little boy imitating old country music, good job.*"

This was fair enough, as a personal opinion, and a fairly common one, but still wrong.

"I forgive you," I said.

"Here's some corny shit I *do* love," she said. She sang along to the opening lines of the John Prine CD she'd inserted: "When I woke up this morning, things were looking bad . . ."

"This *definitely* isn't any better," I said.

"You have got to be honest, about how you feel," she said, echoing the melody of "Illegal Smile." "Otherwise you'll find yourself, unable to deal. My friends in Missoula had a John Prine cover band. The only song they ever played was that one that goes 'Pretty good, not bad, can't complaaain.' It's kind of a fucked-up song?"

"For sure," I said.

When we took the fork at the country convenience store near Kenny's house, Kiki got excited and started pacing in the backseat. I cracked one of the back windows and she stuck her head out, nose twitching like crazy. We pulled into the long, densely forested driveway and Kiki lost it, trying to jam her entire thick body through the tiny window crack. When we'd gotten halfway up the drive, I stopped and let her jump out. She raced up ahead of the car and into the trees, already on the trail of some phantom deer.

"Is she okay doing that?" Leslie said.

"Usually," I said. "I've only lost her a couple times out here. She's always made it back eventually. As you see."

We parked in front of the house and Kiki came tearing across the meadow toward us, her sloppy tongue nearly to the ground. She sniffed wildly at the front steps, then did a lap around the house. She marched up to me with an interrogative head tilt.

"I know, little Scruggs isn't here, Keek," I said. "Kenny took him to New Hampshire."

She raced around the side of the house to the shady mud-hole where the tadpoles lived. Usually I tried to keep her out of there, because it was disgusting, but since she'd be outside all day anyway I let it go. Dog wanted to get covered in slime and eat frog babies? Today was her lucky day.

"This is a sweet spot," Leslie said.

"You'd really like Kenny," I said. "He's, like, the opposite of me in a lot of ways. He's the best."

"What does that make you?" Leslie said. "Do you think I'd like him better?"

"Well, he's really tall," I said. "So you'd have that in common."

She was wearing a nearly translucent purple Western shirt, unbuttoned over a black one-piece bathing suit and pink cutoff jean shorts. Now that we were out here in the middle of nowhere, alone in goddamn bucolic splendor with a cooler full of beer, I fully admitted to myself that I badly wanted to have sex with Leslie, and started working through whether or not I was going to commit myself to actually trying to do that. My hope, as always, was that someone else would make the decision for me, absolve me of the little responsibility I had. One thing I've learned: you can always—always—have less responsibility.

We walked out to the chicken coop behind the house, past the garden sprawling with basil and mint and deer skulls. I nearly kicked Kiki trying to keep her out of the coop—I didn't trust her around chickens since an unfortunate Sunday brunch at which she'd been caught at the pond with a drowned orange bantam hen in her mouth. Julia swore she'd been framed, but I saw the murder in her eyes. Kenny'd forgiven me after I presided over a chicken burial, but if she killed another one, I doubted either of us would be as easily absolved.

"Do you know anything about chickens?" Leslie said. The coop was terribly hot, multiplying the smell of straw and bird shit exponentially. I picked up a chopped milk carton full of grain and opened the wire mesh pen. The little dinosaurs rushed us while Kiki howled in frustration outside.

"I think it might turn out you don't *have* to know anything?" I said. "It seems like you just give them food and water, and they lay eggs, and then they get killed by foxes no matter what you do."

"Old MacDonald couldn't have explained it better," she said.

Leslie followed me in and collected the eggs, a couple for each of the three surviving chickens, two of which were regular size, that is, gigantic, and one miniature. The rooster was also tiny, purchased, I believe, to make jokes about having a tiny cock.

After the oppressive claustrophobia of the chicken shack, even the evil humidity of the air outside felt good. We brought the eggs into the dusty kitchen for safekeeping, and I changed into my bathing suit in one of the unused downstairs bedrooms occupied by a rusty metal bedframe and some broken-looking acoustic guitars. When I emerged into the living room, Leslie was standing in front of the woodstove reading an old *New Yorker*.

"This is the one with Henry Lake in it," she said.

Lake was a cautionary tale. He'd made his way through the experimental ranks, publishing flashy, glib stuff in small journals. The legend—apocryphal or not—went that when he finally had a story accepted by *The New Yorker*, he got so distracted reading the email on his phone that he drove his car into a tree. The story itself, published posthumously, was okay, not great. It turned out *The New Yorker* was just a tool, like a gun.

"You want to swim?" I said.

"*Hell* yeah," she said. "You know, this story isn't actually that bad so far."

"It gets worse," I said.

She rolled up the magazine and carried it down to the pond with her. I'd brought a Renata Adler book about an endless lawsuit—it was like I was *trying* to never finish another thing. We picked our way down an overgrown path to the little weather-beaten dock, me with the cooler, Leslie with a stack of towels, Kiki with a fetid tennis ball she'd found in the field. I'd spent many afternoons down here with Kenny, drinking beer and pad-dling lazily across the water's sun-warmed surface and abrupt cold patches. I admired Leslie's collarbone bulging under the glossy, taut material of her swimsuit. She went to the edge of the dock and dipped her toe in the water.

"Not that cold," she said.

I stuck my foot in and she lunged like she was going to push me. She must have seen terror on my face because she grabbed my hand and pulled me toward her.

"Sorry sorry sorry," she said. "I don't know why I did that."

"It would've been okay," I said.

"Yeah, right, you'd've never've forgiven me," Leslie said. "That would've been the end of it."

"The end of what?"

"I just know you're the kind of person who holds a grudge."

"No, I forgive. I forget."

"I guess the drinking probably helps," she said.

I took a beer out of the cooler, opened it, and took a sip. "I forgive you."

Leslie took a beer, too, and sat on the edge of the dock with her feet in the water. She leaned back so that I was standing over her and looking straight down at her backward face.

"I should really be working," she said with exaggerated languor.

"I think this counts," I said. "It's like walking the dog."

"Right, right," she said, still languid, but distracted. "I mean, where does people's energy come from?"

"Rage, I guess? Sexual dysfunction?"

She put a folded towel under her head and blocked the sun with her magazine. I lay perpendicular to her across the dock, trying, barely, to follow Adler's ridiculously thorough discussion of libel law, but mostly noticing how hot I was getting and wondering where Kiki had run off to and imagining what part of the Lake story Leslie was reading at any given second. Finally I couldn't stand my restlessness anymore. I pulled my shirt off—she'd have to see my torso flab at some point—and dived shallowly into the pond. Okay, it was cold. Kiki suddenly appeared on the far bank of the pond, running back and forth in her usual riot of competing emotions—Jump in and save Dad? Bark frantically to alert him of the danger he faces in the uncharted depths? Remind everyone about the tennis ball that is yet unthrown?

I swam a full loop of the pond, then treaded water by the dock.

"Oh, hello," Leslie said. "It's a wild sea monkey."

"Monkey . . . do?" I said.

"All right, so I guess that story is pretty lame. The main thing about it is that it's just completely average. Certainly not worth *dying* for."

"I didn't know the guy," I said. "Did you hear about the girl who published the same exact story in three different magazines, changing only the proper names and the characters' taste in music?"

"I liked all of them," Leslie said. "Didn't bother me."

"You going to swim?"

"Maybe when I finish this beer. And yours. It's getting cooked."

"Send it here."

Now *that* was cool—swimming and drinking beer at the same time. Actually I was mostly just holding on to the dock while gulping it, and the beer was disgustingly warm. I finished it and grabbed Leslie's ankle, tugged on it gently.

"All's fair, but I do *not* want splinters in my ass," she said.

I lifted her foot—the one I'd been admiring during the movie, or the other one—and kissed the tops of her toes.

"Oh, I see," she said. "I see."

I lifted her other foot and got to those toes, too.

"Well, that's all of them," she said, smiling down at me.

I covered my face and went underwater in mostly mock shame, reemerging some twenty feet away from the dock.

"What happened?" she called. "Come back here."

That was what I needed, like a vampire. I swam underwater toward her and popped up near her legs.

"Do you want me to drown you?" Leslie said.

"Is that my only option?"

"Come up here," she said.

I hoisted myself up none too gracefully by the elbows and sat next to her, facing the water. I put my hand on her tan, bare thigh and her eyes presented me with a blunt question. I was trying, unsuccessfully, to answer *yes* with mine, but luckily she just pulled me down on top of her.

"Sorry I'm so wet," I mumbled. She bit my bottom lip and felt around inside my bathing suit. I lunged to kiss her and the back of her head thunked lightly against the dock.

"Is this cool?" she said.

I ran my hand down her front, which was hot from an hour of afternoon sun.

"Let's get this thing off of you," I said. I pulled down the straps of her suit and wrenched the rest of it crackling down her body and off. I felt momentarily embarrassed by the vulnerability of her undersunned breasts, and shifted my gaze to her dark legs.

I kissed her thighs, swallowed sunscreen. She sat up and tugged at the waist of my shorts, so I released the knot of the drawstring and slid them off. I loomed over her on my knees, moved my fingers inside her gently. It was incredibly bright out, so bright that the glare off the water hurt my eyes, and I closed them to her twitching flesh.

"How prepared are you to fuck me?" Leslie said after a few minutes of this.

"Oh," I said. "I mean. I don't . . . have anything? But I'm good. I mean, uh, safe? What about you?"

"That's not how it works," Leslie said. She stood up and walked over to the grass, pulled an opened box of condoms out of her bag. She tore one package off from the line of six.

"You should take this as a real compliment," she said.

When I pushed into her she gave a low grunt, so different from Julia's pitched murmurings that I worried I'd hurt her. But she was with me, with it, driving me deeper into her with throat sounds of affirmation. It'd been a while since I'd worn a condom, and I found myself thinking like a teenager—Was it still on? Had it broken? Leslie didn't seem worried.

"I haven't had a cock in me for a *month*," she said. "What the *fuck*?"

We rolled over. I was acutely aware of how much bigger she was than Julia, of how the length of her body negotiating mine felt like a wrestling match. With her on top of me, my back and shoulders started aching within seconds—Leslie'd managed a long time against the dock without complaining.

"*Here* we are," she said. "This is how we finish."

She touched herself and pressed down hard against me, and it was the sound of her crying out, a sudden, emphatic "Oh *shit*" coupled with her palm slamming into my chest, that startled me into coming, too. She delicately extricated herself and lay flat against me. We reeked of sunscreen and oniony sweat and rubber. She bumped her forehead against mine so that we were nose to nose and her sweaty hair made a curtain over my face. I couldn't see her.

"Boy, this is *fun*," she drawled. "And you're not that bad a lay."

Even couched in such a way, I felt, as she'd known I would, inordinately proud of this. It's hard to know *what* kind of lay you are when you've been with the same person for as long as I had been. I did think of Julia now, though that was about as far as it went: her name fading up into my mind intermittently, then fading back down, without her face or any particular emotion attached. Its very presence implied guilt, but I didn't really feel it yet.

We lay next to each other side by side, taking on sun. There was, in me at least, the intuition that when we broke this self-conscious idyll—gathered our clothes and reading material and trash, found the dog, tromped back up the path through the trees to the house—the next, more difficult part of our comradeship would commence, one defined by tension and secrecy and lies. But: it didn't. We said some funny things to each other as we trundled through our tasks, threw a hopelessly muddy Kiki in the wayback of the car, and rapped along to Drake on the radio as we drove back into town. I dropped her at her aunt's, kissed her, glowing, on the mouth, and drove home. I drank a beer in the shower humming that John Prine song—"pretty good, not bad, can't complain." When Julia got home, I was making dinner—black beans and rice, but still—for once in my god-damn life.

Part II

When Leslie was twenty-five, she lived in New York and, for longer than she should have, dated Todd. Todd was a playwright and actor who held down a day job at an investment firm, the one that prided itself on hiring artistic types for their ability to "think outside the box." Maybe unsurprisingly, given the amount of work he was expected to do, Todd was deeply reliant on Adderall, and, in the quantities he took it, combined with never eating and also drinking a great deal, he became, not infrequently, an insane person. He wasn't terrifically pleasant to begin with—that wasn't the attraction, exactly—but by the end of a week in which he'd worked five ten-hour days at the office and then stayed up most of the nights writing and snorting speed, he was demonic, insisting he was imbued with powers greater than those of "lazy, weak-minded hipsters." Never mind, or perhaps take into account, the fact that he was five foot eight and rail thin, a bald, chain-smoking skeleton.

His play about "the shadow cabinet" of George W. Bush, in which the torture victims of history (early Christian martyrs, Armenians, Cambodians) assemble in the Situation Room to approve war crimes, was kind of funny, mostly disturbing. Todd himself played the president, though he spoke in his own voice and didn't wear a suit, instead sporting a white undershirt with "prezident" scrawled across it in Sharpie. Leslie attended a weekend's worth of performances of this play only a month after meeting him, and even though the show was pretty awful, she saw the potential, or was at least willing to see where things went. It became clear to her that first weekend that he and his female producer Katie were also sleeping together, but it didn't overly bother her. She knew from a brief college career acting in an anything-goes Shakespeare troupe that theater people were going to do what they wanted, common decency be damned. There was no stopping what happened backstage.

Sex with Todd was a mess. Between the drugs and his anxiety and his selfishness, there wasn't a lot to work with. He wanted to be "the dominant one," a preference with which Leslie was happy to comply, though the fact that she was taller, heavier, and stronger than him created something of a sight gag when she mentally removed herself from the scene, which happened frequently during the periods in which she was nominally restrained in some way and he was trying to get an erection by stringing together long sequences of vulgarities and slapping himself in the face. When she was allowed to take control of their sexual activities, ordering him to do this or that, he came almost immediately, which was unfortunately more a source of shame and disappointment to him than pleasure. The only times *she* got to come were when she "made him" go down on her, which he did reluctantly and badly. And yet, he still turned her on, somehow, at least in principle. When they were apart, she sometimes touched herself thinking about him. The *idea* of him, not *him* him.

Him him told her that a short story she'd written was "a really nice first effort" and that she should come back to it once she'd read some of the books he thought she'd find useful. (She had not, at this point, made it very far in *Mason & Dixon*.) She got drunk for courage and emailed the story anyway to a friend who worked at an important magazine, asking him only to tell her she wasn't crazy for thinking it wasn't bad. In response, she got a note from the fiction editor a week later, saying that the story was "brilliantly conceived, if not entirely emotionally coherent," and that while they couldn't take it, they'd be interested to see more work in the future. It shook her so deeply that she didn't write a word of fiction for over a year. She didn't tell Todd about any of it.

One night, she and Todd and his producer Katie were out late at a bar near Katie's apartment in Park Slope, drinking endless whiskeys and taking turns doing Todd's cocaine in the bathroom. Katie had the open, helplessly expressive face of a Northern Renaissance Madonna, sad and shining with inner knowledge. While Todd was occupied with his drugs, Katie nuzzled her head against Leslie's shoulder.

"You should stay over my place tonight," she said. "It's gonna take you forever to get home from here."

"Would that be okay?" Leslie said. She hated paying for cars, on principle, and couldn't really afford them, either. Ride-sharing was still but a glimmer in a young misogynist's eye.

Katie lifted her head from Leslie's shoulder and nodded solemnly.

"I want your company," she said. "'Cause I'm a *sad* and *looonely* girl."

"What happened to what's-his-name? Charles?"

"Charles *sucked*. Bad talker. Better to be alone."

"Hey, did you and Todd ever, like, *date* date?" Leslie said.

"Nooooo, no no," Katie said. "I mean, we have *history*, certainly. And I love him to death. But I couldn't deal with that, like, consistently. Not that you shouldn't."

They watched him walk across the room, stopping at the bar to order another drink.

"He *is* charming sometimes," Leslie said.

"I know, believe me," Katie said. "Too bad—for all of us, really—that he's so shite in bed. Unlike you, I bet."

Leslie, seized by some combination of relief, despair, and desire, leaned over and bit Katie on the neck, twisting her mouth as she disengaged to leave a mark.

"*Oh*, I see, you're an *animal*," Katie said.

Leslie made a low growling sound, like a dog.

"You be *good*," Katie said, petting Leslie's hair.

Leslie was panting and holding her wrists limp like paws when Todd returned to the table.

"One thing you can never have too much of?" Todd said. "Whiskey and cocaine."

Leslie leaned over the table and licked his face in a long slurp.

"Now *that's* the kind of affection I'm looking for," he said. "Just bypassing cerebral consideration and honing right in on the salt of human skin."

Leslie gave a demure howl and finished her drink.

"Sir, you can't just bring a dog into a bar," Katie said.

"Aw, she's house-trained," Todd said.

Leslie thought for a moment about pissing herself in order to enter the realm of legend, but she worried she was too drunk to plausibly claim it had been fully intentional, and not quite drunk enough to make herself that uncomfortable on so many levels.

"Look what she did," Katie said, showing Todd her neck.

"Oh *shit*," Todd said. "Okay. Now I've got a better picture of this whole situation."

"The puppy and I were thinking we should all go back to my place."

Leslie lowered her face to Todd's drink and lapped some whiskey out with her tongue. It was surprisingly difficult to get

much down your gullet that way. She hadn't realized Todd would
be invited for whatever this next thing was.

"I *do* have a couple more songs coming up on the jukebox . . ."
Todd said. The bar didn't have a jukebox. He finished his drink
in two long gulps and crunched on some ice as he stood up. The
two women followed him out the door.

By the time they'd walked the four blocks to Katie's, and up
the three flights of stairs to her apartment, Leslie had sobered
up a little bit, and wondered about what they were thinking here
exactly. But then they each had another good-size line to finish
off Todd's cocaine (the stuff simply didn't *keep*) and she was re-
flooded with enthusiasm. She hadn't realized the degree to which
these months of lousy sex had sharpened her desire, and now that
the possibility of something different was close, she was nauseous
with anticipation, internally begging Todd to be cool, even as
she knew that, even on TV, these kinds of things never seemed
to actually work out.

As Katie poured drinks in the kitchen, Leslie decided that
the only plausible way for her to deal with her anxiety would be
to manifest it, that is, cede control of herself and let the anxiety take her over. In this case: act like an idiot and see if it got
her what she wanted.

"I wanna be in your lap," she mumbled at Todd. She stretched
languidly from her end of the couch onto his, placing her head
where his dick might be.

"Sleepy?" he said.

She rolled her head back and forth slowly. Not sleepy. Something else. She turned her face upward toward his.

"I *like* Katie," she said in a babyish voice.

"Yeah, she's the best," Todd said. "I'd be lost if not for her.
More lost, I mean."

"I wanna play with her."

"Isn't that what we're doing?"

"I mean I wanna . . ." She switched to a whisper. "I wanna *play* with her."

"I got it, Les," he said. "We'll just have to see what happens, won't we?"

She sighed and sat up as Katie came back into the room with the drinks.

"These are Negronis, but they're mostly just Campari," Katie said. "A little dessert nightcap for us good kids."

Leslie took a sip from the one nearest her and shuddered. Campari tasted horrible to her, but she kind of liked it anyway.

"You okay?" Katie said, perched with her legs draped across the arm of an easy chair.

"A little. Strung. *Out*," Leslie said rhythmically. She hunched over and put her fingers to her temples. "I wish. *Someone*. Would kiss me!"

She kept her eyes on the low coffee table, but imagined Katie and Todd exchanging glances, drawing straws. Then there was a hand lifting her chin, and Katie's blurry face pressing into hers. Leslie pulled her down gracelessly, grappling her vaguely toward Todd, too, so that he'd feel involved. She mauled Katie's mouth with her own, pulling at her lips with her teeth while trying to hassle her bodily onto the couch.

"Hey, let me get my boots off," Katie said.

Leslie whimpered and leaned over to kiss Todd's ear. He moved his head just out of her reach, smiling vaguely, his eyes quiet.

"There we go," Katie said, climbing onto the couch in her black-socked feet. She kissed Leslie on the mouth gently, thoroughly, then glanced over at Todd.

"Have at it," he said.

"We want you, too," Leslie said, though she didn't. She pulled on his collar. She ran her hand over his crotch, but nothing seemed to be going on there.

"I'm here," he said.

Katie seemed to not care either way, as she was now putting her hands on any part of Leslie she could reach, and Leslie was inclined to stop worrying about Todd's feelings now, too, what with the sex and substances rolling through her brain. It could all be chalked up to inebriation later, and frankly, at this juncture, it was unclear whether or not she and Todd had much of a future. Leslie let herself be handled, reaching her mouth up for bites and tastes of Katie like a fish coming to the surface of a pond.

"Should we move this whole project to the bedroom?" Katie said.

She stood up and pulled Leslie to her feet.

"Come on, Todd," Leslie said.

"I think I'm going to head home," Todd said. "But you guys should have fun. Seriously."

Katie strode over to him, got in his face.

"You *said* this is what you wanted," she said. "You talk to me all day about how you have these debauched visions or whatever, you think you're fucking *Artaud* or something, and then you don't have any interest in actually *doing* anything. This is just like the night with that Cambridge guy. You get all revved up, you coke yourself into fucking *abstraction*, and then you *bounce*."

"That guy was literally on heroin," Todd said. "And I'm sorry that if, on reflection, I'm actually not that excited about hooking up with my girlfriend and my, you know, *producer* at the same time. Business and pleasure and all that shit that Artaud didn't have to worry about. I'm aware I'm a fucking downer and a fraud and everything else. I'm not, like, thrilled about it."

Leslie remained in the doorway of Katie's bedroom. She really, really did not want to go home with Todd and spend the rest of the night listening to his self-laceration. She really *was* too drunk for that—she would not be able to sufficiently pretend to care.

"It's s'okay, Todd," Leslie said, leaning hard into the slur. "You're just good boy, I know. I'm jus' gonna sleep here, 'kay?"

She stumbled over to the couch and crashed down onto it limply. She was surprised by how quickly her legs came out from under her—she had little springs for knees.

"Don't pretend to be drunk, Les," Todd said. "You're really not good at it."

Leslie got up from the couch and walked more steadily than she'd thought possible into the small kitchen off the living room. She clawed a fistful of ice out of the freezer and dropped it in a tall glass, then filled the glass nearly to the top with gin. She emerged back into the other room brandishing the drink like a gun. She caught Todd's eye, then tipped her head back and poured most of the drink down her throat. It went down surprisingly smoothly, until she stopped chugging and caught the juniper-flavored puke at the back of her tongue, and swallowed it back down.

"What the fuck are you doing?" Todd said, panicky now.

She lifted the glass again and, faster than she could process it, he slapped his hand against hers, hard, sending the glass into the wall and breaking it into heavy pieces on the floor. She walked purposefully into the kitchen and grabbed the bottle of gin out of the freezer, unscrewed it with a flourish while looking straight at Todd, lifted it to her mouth.

"Leslie, Leslie, fuck, stop," Katie said, her eyes on the floor. There was a trail of bright blood between the foyer and kitchen. And there was some serious pain emanating from the soft middle of Leslie's foot, which definitely had something large and sharp embedded in it. She sat down heavily, heard more glass crunch under her denimed ass. She examined her foot, found the source of pain, gaped into the abyss of blood and flesh.

"Okay, Leslie, just stay calm, okay?" Katie's voice came from a distance, fuzzy. She didn't know where Todd was—had he

walked out the door? Had she missed the slam? Calmly, carefully, she tugged the jagged slice of glass from her foot. She
examined it in her hand. It looked artisanal. A hip earring, a
blood diamond, a fat DiCaprio calling out to her with a bad
accent . . .

She woke in the dark, naked except for her underwear,
which, a moment's examination revealed, was not her underwear. There was a folded towel next to her head, unsoiled. Then
she felt an incoming throb from her foot, a pain that built, and
built, and crested, and stayed.

"Ow!" she cried out, like a child on the playground. "Oh,
fuck, ow. Fuck."

"Shhh," Katie said. She was in the bed, too, apparently. A
lamp flicked on. "Did you throw up again?"

"No?" Leslie said. The question scared her. "I don't think so?
Oh god, what did I do?"

"You're okay," Katie said. "You've been having a pretty bad
time. Are you with me now? Do you know where you are?"

"Your apartment? Is that right?"

"Good, yeah, that's right. You got a little bit sick."

"Oh god. What about my foot?"

"I cleaned it up. It stopped bleeding, mostly, but I don't really
know. I think you might need stitches."

As Leslie came to awareness, she realized they were lying
on and under towels spread over a bare mattress, in a bed that
took up most of a small room. Leslie looked down and saw that
there was a plastic shopping bag taped around her foot.

"I'll buy you new sheets," Leslie said. "I'll buy you a new *bed*.
Jesus, I'm so sorry, Katie. I don't know how this happened."

"Things got crazy," Katie said. Her voice was tired, but not
unkind. "And just so you know, Todd left. And hasn't answered
his phone."

"Shit, I hope he's okay," Leslie said. "Let me try." She

looked around for her phone, or anything that belonged to her, and found nothing.

"Your phone is . . . out of commission," Katie said gently. "It's like five a.m. You should try to sleep more if you can, okay?"

Leslie curled into a ball. She wished she had the courage or the resources to die at that moment without causing Katie any more trouble. Katie put her arms around Leslie and pulled her body tight.

"You had a bad night," she murmured. "It happens. It's okay. I know you're not a bad person. I still want to be your friend."

"I'm so sorry," she said quietly, maybe inaudibly.

"You're a good person," Katie said. "You had a bad night. It's going to be okay."

Katie's supportive muttering faded into snores eventually. Once some gray light had filtered into the room, Leslie gently extricated herself from Katie's sleeping grasp and went into the bathroom. Her shirt and jeans—even her *shoes*—were piled in the tub, covered in bright red vomit—what had she *eaten?*— along with some sheets and pillows and a Mondrian-patterned comforter. She extricated her pukey phone from the pocket of her jeans. Had she puked on it and then put it *back* in her pocket? She held down the power button as she peed, trying to force the phone, without success, back into digital consciousness. She was upset, like an idiot, about losing her pictures.

She wrapped a towel around herself and crept into the front room to examine the damage. There was a small dent in the wall where the glass had hit, and faint bloodstains on the kitchen tile, but other than that, it looked okay. She'd write Katie a check, or send her a bunch of money online when she got home. She wished she could just sneak away, but she needed something to wear, and stealing clothes probably wasn't a great finale to this whole debacle. Though, to be honest, it would be one of the *less* bad things she'd done in the last twenty-four hours. She curled up on the couch and fell back asleep.

———

Katie insisted on accompanying her to the ER, even waited with her for the two hours it took before a doctor would see her, reading last weekend's *Times Magazine* while Leslie stared at the blown-up Hieronymus Bosch reproduction on the cover of her book, an upside-down naked couple looking sad and stunned to be trapped in a presumably unpleasant landscape. Good thinking, book jacket designer. It's like the fact that they're upside down echoes the psychological circumstances of the characters.

When a nurse finally called her name, Leslie asked Katie to come in with her, because she was still the tiniest bit needle-phobic, and more than a tiny bit hungover. Maybe, if Katie saw her through all of this, she could be in love with her.

The doctor shook his head unhappily at the sloppy triage done on Leslie's foot.

"You should have come in right away," he said.

"Is it bad?" Leslie said, involuntarily creeping toward panic. "What are you going to do?"

"It's not that bad," he said grudgingly, now that he'd suc-ceeded in scaring her. "The scar's just going to be a little more . . . interesting than it might have been. Sit tight and we'll have somebody come in and stitch you up."

"Why are you being so nice to me?" Leslie said as they waited for the medical student.

Katie crossed her legs, smiled vaguely.

"I don't know you that well," she said. "But it seems like you might need someone looking out for you."

Leslie exhaled, attempted to check her defensiveness.

"I know," she said. "I know I fucked up last night. I'm going to join the Peace Corps and move to Botswana."

"Well I don't want you to do *that*," Katie said.

"Why not?"

"Well, you were pretty amorous last night before everything went to hell," Katie said. "Before it was entirely clear to me that your brain had exited the scene. Or maybe I was taking advantage of you."

"I'm sure I liked it. Did it seem like I liked it?"

"Yeah, until you started vomiting uncontrollably."

"I promise I'm going to buy you some new sheets," Leslie said.

"That's right," Katie said. "And dinner."

"Anything you want," Leslie said. "From the dollar menu."

Then the medical student entered the room, a boy who didn't look a day over seventeen.

"So," he said, stretching on his latex gloves. "What happened here?"

———

They went their separate ways for the afternoon, Leslie promising, after a quick, fluttery kiss, that she'd text her about dinner that night. Maybe that farmy-looking place on Seventh Avenue if it wasn't too jammed? She'd better text, Katie said. Leslie limped toward the subway, not at all sure that she would. She forced her eyes to stay open on the subway so she wouldn't miss her stop, then felt herself nearly falling asleep as she unlocked the front door to her apartment. She did not remember getting into bed, but that was where she was when she woke up, in the dark, an indefinite number of hours later, hungover, again.

She opened her laptop—8:22. She had an email from Katie a couple of hours old. Katie realized that Leslie's phone wasn't working and that she probably needed to rest and that she'd

maybe come on a little bit strong at the hospital and that it made
sense to give her a little bit of space, especially because Leslie
was still dating Todd. But she still really hoped Leslie would get
in touch if she wanted to have food or coffee or see a movie or
something, because she, Katie, would really love that, even if it
didn't lead to anything else or whatever.

Leslie got just a little bit stoned and thought this over. What
did she *want* to do? Like, now? She didn't want to stay in her disgustingly messy room. She didn't want to deal with Todd. She
didn't want to go to her friend Francesca's birthday drinks in
Bushwick. She wanted: to see Katie again, and be high, and treat
Katie to some expensive, delicious food that she couldn't really
afford to buy her but would, as a result, ease her guilt a few degrees, and would feel romantic in its ignorance of her material
circumstances. So she wrote her a quick, flirtatious email, ignoring the Sturm und Drang of Katie's original, asking if she still
wanted to go to that place, Woods, it was called, for dinner,
because *she* hadn't eaten all day and was, frankly, *starving*. Katie
wrote back almost immediately to say yes.

So an hour later, after finally taking a scalding shower and
putting on her go-to black cocktail dress, and writing an old-
fashioned hundred-dollar check that she would try to force Katie
to take later in the night, and getting substantially more stoned
than she already was, she took the subway a few stops to Seventh
Avenue and arrived at the restaurant, only fifteen minutes late.
Which proved to be five minutes before Katie—well played, Katie.

But when Katie finally made her entrance, Leslie realized that
she'd made a mistake. Leslie'd taken care to look respectable,
but Katie was transformed, made-up and cinched and showing
off her legs in a way that indicated she was unmistakably on a date
of import. And the fact that this sharpened Leslie's nascent nau-
sea told her that she had made the wrong choice in inviting Katie
to dinner. Even if things went perfectly, she would remember

having felt a pang of embarrassment for Katie when she walked into the restaurant, even though she looked amazing, like something out of a luxury handbag advertisement. These little fucking *blondes*, man. Leslie's charm, such as it was, tended toward the feral.

"*You're* looking alive," Katie said as she sat down across the candlelit table. The restaurant was very loud, as were all restaurants in New York now.

"A roguish façade," Leslie said. "I'm pretending for you."

"That's nice," Katie said. "You *do* have some manners lurking in there."

"They only come out at night. And only, um, between eight and eleven. Prices and participation may vary."

There was a pause as Katie held a smile, waiting for a further punch line, or an apology.

"You look really, really great, by the way," Leslie said finally.

"Thanks!" Katie said, in the faux-surprised voice that Leslie hated in most people, but now found almost charming, or at least forgivable. "I thought it'd be fun to get dolled up."

"I like it," Leslie said. She was trying to lean into it, into the weed, into possible attraction. "You look a heartbeat away from the presidency."

"Is that a Sarah Palin joke? If so, great job."

"I was thinking of Dick Cheney. As I often am."

Katie looked into Leslie's eyes queryingly, like she was trying to determine whether or not John Malkovich was in there.

"Are you fucked-up?" she said brightly. Maybe Katie was being deeply facetious and was furious at her. Or maybe she was glad to find her pliable again so soon. Leslie tried to smile in a way that didn't make her neck tendons stand out too much.

"I'm staying off the booze for a while," she said. "But you should know, I guess, that I'm usually, like, pretty stoned. More so now from lack of sleep and general whatever. Malaise."

"Understandable," Katie said. "No judgment. Would you be annoyed if *I* had a cocktail? Obviously you should have one, too, if you're up for it."

"I'd enjoy watching you have one," Leslie said. It seemed like the kind of thing an alcoholic lesbian might say.

Katie ordered something with strawberry and basil in it, and Leslie ordered a Diet Coke, which made her think of eating lunch with her mother, accumulating free refills for two hours and thus needing to pee about four times over the course of the meal, which otherwise consisted mostly of her mother criticizing her life choices, or lack of them. Katie so far seemed like the opposite of her mother, which maybe was what women looked for in other women? The only girl she'd *dated* dated had been a boyish poet in college who dressed like a nerd from an eighties movie, all coffee-stained bow ties and heavy glasses held together with tape. Less a disguise, it turned out, than an attempt at manifestation—Becky thought she *was* John Berryman, basically, suicidal ideation and all, and Leslie hadn't minded chasing her around and visiting her in the hospital until, eventually, she gave up in exhaustion. She'd liked Becky enough that she'd tried to explain it to her mother, who had pretended she didn't understand until Leslie got the hint that she didn't want to talk about it. She wondered now if she even *had* tried to tell her mother—could it have been a false memory? She preferred that possibility to the more likely fact of her mother's unkindness.

"What's good to eat here?" Leslie said. "Duck? Ducks are usually tasty."

"I want to get something *expensive*," Katie said. She grinned wolfishly, and Leslie wanted her again, for however long it worked out.

By the end of dinner, Leslie had talked herself into having a cognac for dessert. It was basically a necessity, as the weed had worn off, and she'd felt too hollowed out and nauseous to eat much. It seemed like the only route to getting regular. It did just what she'd hoped it would, warmed her up and sparked her into clarity without making her feel sick or drunk. Thank you, kind elixir! Leslie loved not having a phone—she felt practically snowbound with Katie, stuck in a blizzard of two. When the bill arrived, she did her best to stifle her unhappiness. She absolutely couldn't afford it, but she put her credit card down anyway. It was what she deserved. The closest she'd get to medieval penance.

"It was really sweet of you to do this," Katie said once the boy had whisked away the offending numbers. "It shows, god forbid, *character*."

"I mostly just don't want you to hate me," Leslie said. "Which is pretty selfish."

"Hey, if it results in a good dinner, I'm willing to fudge it. I imagine you're about ready to go back to bed."

"I'm kind of *awake* now. Having slept through the day. Do you want to, like, go to the *movies*? Would that be fun?"

"Oh man, it would, wouldn't it? I wonder if anything's playing."

"I think they're still doing Altman at BAM," Leslie said. She knew they were; she'd looked it up, by habit, before she left. "What is it, Saturday? They usually save the good ones for Saturday." She knew it was *McCabe & Mrs. Miller*, one of her favorite movies, and that it started in twenty minutes. Katie looked it up on her phone—she'd never seen *McCabe & Mrs. Miller*, actually. And it started in twenty minutes.

So they walked to BAM and soaked in the same three Leonard Cohen songs over and over again and Warren Beatty's incomprehensible muttering and Julie Christie's feline perfection, and Leslie felt happier than she had in a long time, with Katie sighing next to her in the dark. When they said good night—Leslie couldn't deal with returning to Katie's, the scene of the crime, so soon, and her own place was too disgusting to host another human—Leslie gave her a serious kiss. This—this could work, she thought.

Three nights later, they hooked up for real back at Katie's house, on the new plaid sheets she'd bought with the money that Leslie had given her. It was wonderful to remember that things did *not* have to be as difficult as they'd been with Todd, that of course two people with sexual chemistry could please each other quite adequately. Katie was even smaller than Todd in every way, so Leslie still felt like something of a giantess. But with Katie she felt more powerful than awkward, even if she still, inevitably, felt a little bit awkward.

They were very different kinds of women, it seemed to Leslie, besides the basics of them both being artistic and drunk and broke. Katie, unlike Leslie, was not simply tumbling through her life. She'd gotten a master's degree in theater arts at NYU, somehow paid her own rent, cooked frequently, showered as often, apparently, as once a day. She had an actual television. Leslie mostly found this stuff a turn-on, though it also gave her pause. She suspected that Katie didn't really understand what a disaster she was, and didn't understand that Leslie was actively taking notes on her, greedily excited to have someone she didn't understand to investigate.

One night, as a date, maybe, Leslie took Katie to a punk show headlined by a band she loved, one whose name was unprintable in *The New York Times*. They'd both gotten very stoned on intense stuff that had been inadvisably mailed from Denver (Leslie was still pretending she wasn't going to drink much anymore), and the opening band that was playing when they walked in—a very thin woman shaking a metal trash can full of what sounded like tin and marbles—was too much to handle in their condition. They stood at the quiet bar downstairs drinking water and staring at the bloodred wall behind the tiered liquor bottles.

"Shit, I don't think I even asked if you *liked* punk rock," Leslie said.

"Yeah, I guess I don't, really," Katie said. "But I figured it would be fun."

Leslie put her hand on Katie's back, pressed against it gently.

"You're a true comrade," she said. "When the revolution comes, I will spare you. If I can."

Katie gave her a stoned, deadpan glare. "You must convince the others. I am a good person."

"If I cannot, we will run away. Together."

Katie kissed her, and then put her head on Leslie's shoulder. Their sleepiness and laziness did not bode well for the upcoming hours of heedless mayhem, but they could probably rally. And maybe that was the way adults *should* experience punk rock anyway. Observe and assimilate rather than take a direct role in the destruction. Were they adults? Leslie was twenty-five. Katie would soon be thirty. Hard to say.

When her beloved band came on, they watched the set from the back of the room, Leslie resisting, barely, the urge to rush the stage. She imagined she was storing the energy from the room for later, for fucking. When they got home, however, the action leaned closer to soft rock than hardcore.

Something similar, but worse, happened a couple of weeks later. They took the train out to see an exhibition of Sol LeWitt drawings at an art museum in the Hudson Valley. In Leslie's conception of herself, Sol LeWitt was one of her favorite artists, someone who, through his conceptual practice, embodied some kind of defiance that she found appealing. And she found his stuff nice to look at, too, soothing in its repetition and formality. She was, in general, a sucker for minimalism, in both its quietest and most imposing forms. She worried that it might be because it echoed some fundamental emptiness at the heart of her idea of things, some inability to understand and process the world in all its richness and complexity. It was easy to say that art was all [this] when you couldn't conceive of anything beyond [this].

When they got there, Katie pronounced the whole thing tedious, and Leslie, partly because of her influence, and partly because of her own unpredictable swings in patience and taste, was left antsy and underwhelmed, too, and the low-hanging gray sky and galleries packed with well-to-do, superficially satisfied patrons didn't help either. They wandered through the permanent collection, Leslie mostly frustrated by her own frustration. Katie seemed bemused, but happy enough. Whatever the problems in play, they were mostly Leslie's. They stopped in a room filled with paintings by On Kawara, whose work had always left Leslie cold. The paintings in this room all consisted of white letters and numbers, identifying the date on which they were painted, on uniform black, rectangular canvases. Leslie was expecting to not give a shit as usual, but instead she felt an overwhelming sadness flooding into her chest. These things were a monument to . . . what? The reading pushed by the wall panel was something about the inevitability of time, the inability of humans to freeze it or memorialize it effectively. Somehow, the wall panel thought, painting the date every day for forty years or whatever had a cumulatively devastating effect, like reading an epic autobiographical novel. But, Jesus, could On Kawara, even if he was the bleakest motherfucker on earth, really think that he was capturing his story in full? That he was capturing anything at all? Maybe, if you were looking from space, it was enough to see that someone had said, I'm here, I'm here. But she was on earth. She was here, too.

"Do you like these?" Katie asked. She seemed genuinely curious.

"I think I hate them," Leslie said. "But it might just be me."

"Yeah," Katie said. She put her arm around Leslie's shoulder. They were standing in front of OCT. 31, 1978. "It's like looking in a mirror."

———

They took the train back without talking much. Katie was going to a dinner party to which Leslie had not been explicitly invited, though Katie had insisted repeatedly that she was welcome. Leslie didn't feel welcome, though she recognized that this was, again, mostly her problem. Wasn't alienation always your own fault? People were what they were. You could either get in line and find a way to make it work or be a soul adrift upon the wandering etc. People could surprise you. People were interesting. The problem was you.

So on her way from the subway to her apartment, she bought a bottle of Buffalo Trace—if she was going to get shitty for the first time in months, she might as well do it on something she *liked*. At home she poured herself a tumbler, neat, and sipped it fastidiously, and then not fastidiously, while reading a collection of art criticism by a writer she approved of, despite his conservative taste. She didn't mind reading about Goya's portraits for the millionth time, or Velázquez's brushstrokes, or Piero's transcendent stillness. It opened her brain up in a way that contemporary art could not, made her generous like school had said art should make her. She got drunker and slowly read a piece about Bonnard—fucking *Bonnard*!—and realized, or decided that she'd realized, that she should learn art history, really *learn* it. *That* was something she could imagine spending some time on, time that wouldn't be, or at least feel, so wasted. Though the whole idea of *wasting time* felt to her like the usual accusatory capitalist horseshit that made everything in the world depressing and pointless. Not that she didn't want *money*. But, like lots of people she knew, she mostly wanted it so she wouldn't have to want it anymore, so that people would get off her back about how she didn't have any. They'd get on her back about something else, though. *They.* The people who were mildly on her back—her family, a couple of her friends—usually went away after a childish, screaming request to be left alone. And then what? Back to intricately imagined fantasies of persecution in the company of no one.

She wanted to get out of New York—right, who didn't? In her internal monologue of escape, the Mountain West held a place of pride, Montana in particular. It was a little bit because of Merle Haggard, but also because one of Leslie's friends, Edward, had once moved to the hinterlands of western Montana when he got a book contract. Though he'd failed to complete, or possibly even begin, his book of comedic essays, he came back with a patchy beard and boundless enthusiasm for Missoula, where the biggest political questions had to do with the killing and sparing of bears and wolves. She'd been surprised by the pang that the idea of the place gave her. She didn't think of herself as a romantic about location, even though she was secretly romantic about everything.

Now she texted Edward. These days, he wrote scripts for and occasionally acted in anarchic Internet videos for a satirical website. He was overwhelmingly cynical, so much so that, like Leslie, he came out on the other side to sincerity. He thought the government and the media and most people were so corrupt as to be unworthy of consideration, but found devotional solace in obscure Trojan Records cuts and stand-up routines and movies where the lengthily elaborated joke was that there was no joke. He spent a lot of time on drugs, listening to music in the company of middle school chums and ex-lovers. And he lived ten blocks away from Leslie. Lo and behold, he was down to hang. His place? She gulped another drink quickly while changing

into rumpled, slightly cleaner clothes than the ones she'd been
wearing.

When her face hit the air outside, she got a better sense of
how gone she was. It required conscious effort not to careen all
over the sidewalk. She lived in the still mostly black part of the
neighborhood—the walk to Edward's was a journey through
gentrification, the upshot being that the booze was wreaking
gradual havoc on her nervous system, and she was more embarrassed to be drunk around her older black neighbors, who she
imagined already disapproved of her, than around the young
white people who roamed Edward's block. Eventually she found
herself swaying in front of the buzzers at Edward's building and
not remembering which one to press. She dimly recalled that his
buzzer was broken anyway, and that, at least as of a year ago,
this necessitated him throwing the key out of the window at
her, and then, when that inevitably led to the key getting lost in
the gutter or the bushes, him having to come down and help her
find it anyway. So she remembered this and went into her texts
to call him, but somehow managed to call Katie instead, and
didn't realize this until Katie answered on about the fifth ring,
saying, "Hey, silly, did you decide you wanted to stop by?" And
Leslie was confused and then immediately annoyed with herself,
and blurted, "*No*," to which Katie chirpily, grimly responded,
"Okay, well, I'm still at the party, gotta go!" and hung up. So
now Leslie felt both guiltier and more in need of comforting
than she had been a few minutes earlier, which was a pretty bad
combination usually, and especially so when she'd had this much
to drink and had concrete plans to drink more. She texted Katie
back: "Sorry love, a misdial of the ♥. See u soon I hope." Then
she actually called Edward and it turned out his buzzer worked
now. 3G. As she ascended the stairs, she got a text from Katie.
"OK dear, cant help but wonder who you meant 2 b calling at
this hour but trust u to make good choices. kind of." Which was

pretty passive-aggressive, or, actually, just aggressive, and it would have annoyed her more if she didn't deserve it. But *Katie* didn't know she deserved it, so Leslie had the *right* to be pissed at her, even if, maybe, Katie knew her well enough by now to know she wasn't up to anything good. And if *that* was the case, it was infuriating in its own right—why did she have to advertise her unsuitability so baldly? Why was there nothing goddamn mysterious about her, like there was about everyone else? Why were even her adventures so cramped and circumscribed? She opened Edward's door without knocking. He was sitting in the living room under his thrift store reproduction of Winslow Homer's shark painting, the one with the lonesome black man in a fishing boat out in the middle of the ocean, surrounded by cartoonish but very threatening sharks. The guy in the picture didn't look that worried, like he knew, maybe, that it was only a painting, which made it secretly postmodern in Leslie's mind. You couldn't write or paint anything after 1900 without acknowledging the frame, right? She knew, because she'd looked it up, that the shark painting, the original of it, was from 1899.

"You made it," Edward said.

"I'm here now," Leslie said.

"You been drankin'?" he said.

"I hadn't been, so that's probably why I'm so . . . drunk." She flopped down onto the couch.

"I'm going to get you some water," Edward said.

"Thank you," Leslie croaked. She had the spins, which wasn't typical for her, but she really *hadn't* been drinking lately, and maybe tolerance wasn't a myth after all. She took the water he gave her in a long, slow gulp and felt a little bit better.

"Lassie? Can you speak, girl?" Edward said after a solid twenty seconds of her staring at the wall trying to focus her eyes. Had she actually turned into a dog recently?

"Cat's in the well?" she said. "Isn't *that* a dumb Dylan song."

"And she's back!" Edward said.

"Buh," she spit. "Well, I'm glad to see you, I guess. I think that's why I came over."

"How can I make your difficult life more tolerable?"

"Just be nice to me, I guess? My brain doesn't work."

"Here, listen to this song me and the boys recorded."

A thin funk jam pulsed from the giant speakers on the floor, someone screaming about ketamine over repetitive guitar scratching.

"Are you *trying* to make me throw up?"

Edward wandered around the room bobbing his head like a chicken. When the song finally ended after what felt like half an hour, the speakers buzzed with ambient unease. He kneeled in front of a record crate, selected something, and dropped the needle on the turntable. Unintelligible dub shouting shook the floor.

"What are you calling your song?" Leslie said.

"Capitalist decadence meets the Technicolor *ooze*," he said without hesitation. "So, what, you're having trouble with *the man*? Got those *midstage pseudo-relationship blues*?"

Half the things Edward said sounded, in both content and tone of voice, like something from a commercial playing on a television in the background of a cartoon.

"Basically," she said. "I'm seeing this cool girl who I probably don't like enough."

Edward sighed in commiseration.

"Do you think I should move to, like, Montana and become a writer?" she said.

He stroked his chin, in parody, mostly, but it looked like he was really thinking.

"I don't see why not," he said. "You hate it, come back."

He took a long hit from a big metal piece that looked like a plumber's tool.

"Thank you," she said. She was grateful to him for taking her seriously. But:

"But won't you miss me?"

He exhaled a cloud of smoke through his nostrils.

"I already do," he said.

He handed over the piece, heavy and cool to the touch, and she took it from him without partaking.

"You don't think I'm just some dummy, right?" she said.

He reached over and patted her on the head.

"You're a very particular, *specific* dummy," he said. "I'd know you anywhere."

Leslie squeezed her knees to her chest and put her chin on her knees, like she was looking over a little wall made out of herself. The dub echoes were, as if by design, giving her a splitting headache.

"Can we listen to something *nice*?" Leslie said. "Wouldn't it be nice to just listen to something *nice* on your fancy speakers?"

He sighed theatrically and hoisted himself to his feet. He flipped through the record box again.

"What is nice, do you think?" he said.

"You *know* what I mean," she said. "Actually, you know, I'm not going to direct you. Let's see what *you* think a nice record is."

He grunted and flipped, then chose something.

"This isn't going to be a this-record-will-change-your-life moment," he said. The opening notes of "Astral Weeks" floated toward them.

"You got it," Leslie said. "Comfort isn't supposed to be transcendent. I'll take that weed now, please."

"It's right next to you," he said.

And so it was.

Leslie felt significantly less despair as time crawled forward.

They listened to gentle shit from the sixties and came up with stupid ideas for videos, short stories, plays. (*Robot Family* was definitely going to be a hit.) She ignored a late call from Katie. By two a.m., she was sprawled across Edward's chest, her hips unsubtly shifting over his pelvis in periodic attempts to "get comfortable." When they inevitably had sex in his room, in complete darkness, she was the aggressor, or at least that was the word that ran through her mind as she sought and encouraged his dick. Though it had been only a few months since she'd last had sex with Todd, a recurrent thought in her stoned mind for the past few hours had been whether or not it would be somehow difficult or unwieldy to deal with a man after spending so much time with Katie. But, she recalled as things progressed, she and Edward had always shared an understanding that extended to bed. They could fuck like they were continuing a conversation, without the anxiety and ritual that attended most such encounters. This meant, at least for her, that they couldn't reach the heights of great, specifically memorable sex that one always hoped for. But it seemed a worthwhile tradeoff in this case, to have his easeful weight bearing down on her. It was particularly satisfying, once they settled into her preferred position, to be powerfully and somewhat carelessly acted upon, until a definite conclusion was reached.

She was leaving town, she decided, staring at the glow-in-the-dark stars on Edward's ceiling. Maybe somewhere else she'd be able to hear herself think, or, failing that, get some fucking writing done.

Part III

From Monday to Friday, Leslie and I spent our days out at Kenny's. We quickly abandoned the pretense that we were only going there as often as necessary for the chores—I left to pick Leslie up before nine a.m., and dropped her off a half hour or so before the end of the workday. That first Monday was overcast, then storming, so we stayed in the house and played with the kitten, letting him race around the house as fast as he could manage with his three legs. Kiki, after her initial enthusiasm for him was greeted with a bloody swipe across the nose from a tiny claw, noted his comings and goings forlornly from a corner. We sat in the shadowy living room watching the rain crash in sheets against the big windows, listening to Kenny's country records and reading. I'd finally found a book that held my interest—*The Executioner's Song*, of all things. I knew that it was tied up in the joy of our lost weekending, but I loved that book like I'd loved *The Call of the Wild* as a kid, like I'd devoured *The Swiss Family Robinson*. I wanted to know every goddamn thing about these people, and thank Christ, the book was a thousand pages long. Leslie was reading *Fools Crow* by James Welch, "for some freaking balance" after *Blood Meridian*, but it seemed to be slow going. Whenever I cackled or exclaimed in surprise, she asked "What?" and I read her the line. Soon enough I was delivering paragraphs, then pages, and then we were alternating, taking breaks for beers when our throats got sore. We were both in love with Nicole Baker, so fucked-up and voracious, naïve but knowing. It seemed impossible that Mailer hadn't made her up (and I guess a few other people have wondered about that, too). Leslie toyed with me off and on all afternoon, like a cat, but didn't let me come until we were halfway out the door, when she finally sucked my cock in the foyer with what felt like one well-calibrated, continuous motion.

Some afternoons I tried to work, mostly moving commas around on three-year-old stories, while Leslie stared pointedly into her computer screen, not typing. She had abandoned the screenplay she'd supposedly been working on after the friends she was writing it for told her that their main potential backer—a young app developer—had been indicted for securities fraud. Now, she said, she was focused on fiction. (So focused that she currently seemed in danger of boring a hole in her laptop screen with her eyes.)

When it was sunny we took long walks around the property, and I recited half-remembered history that Kenny'd told me, much of it probably made-up, about the family that had lived and died there, their hopes and dreams and heights and weights. We absorbed splinters out on the dock, in our knees, hands, elsewhere. We fucked around in the water, fucked, once, in the wet, thick-pebbled dirt.

If I say I didn't worry about it that much, Julia-wise, it was circumstance rather than carelessness. In that place, in that context, Leslie and I were simply *together*, a couple of rapacious friends with space to ourselves. Later, of course, that week took on a great deal of significance, proof that it was possible that things could be perfect between us, but the fact is, things could have been perfect between many combinations of reasonable people in that place, in that situation. It was a paradisiacal trap.

When Kenny finally came home, a week after he said he would, I felt some relief. It felt like leaving the poker table before you'd lost all your money—not a win, necessarily, but it could have been worse.

Also, Brian, Leslie's fiancé, was coming. Julia and I had foolishly committed to having dinner with the two of them on his second night in town, at the fancy tapas restaurant. Leslie claimed it was essential that we meet each other—she'd talked about me too much to him, and he needed to see, in person, that I wasn't a threat. This very nearly made sense.

Every time Leslie talked about Brian, I felt depression gnaw into me. In the days between Kenny's return and Brian's arrival, I spent a lot of time listening to the Sonic Youth albums from their scary period—*Sister*, *EVOL*—songs about killing and being very nervous. They sounded like traveling on an interstate bus at night. Julia was used to me falling into periods of shallow darkness. She made sure I wasn't contemplating imminent self-harm and let me be.

Leslie remained more vocally ambivalent about Brian during our triumphant days than I would have expected or appreciated. She seemed to see little disjunction in idly wondering about whether or not she was going to marry him while we floated around the pond naked after having sex, though, to be fair, I guess I was unapologetically going home to my girlfriend every evening. I'm not saying my unhappiness was calculated for logical consistency, just that it existed.

When the day of our big dinner arrived, I'd been fully transformed into a tightened muscle of absolute tension, barely able to communicate even with myself. The day's class was exhausting. I let the students do group work that devolved quickly into institutional gossip and insults while I met individually with the women about their forthcoming research essays. This mostly consisted of hearing out perfectly legitimate complaints regarding the prison library and its dearth of books about the inequities of the criminal justice system, or anything much else, for that matter. I promised I'd bring some back issues of *Dissent* and *n+1*. The last hour of the class was dedicated to all of us finally turning on the woman who continued to insist she wasn't a white supremacist, despite the fact that she wanted to write her paper about the threat posed by the worldwide weakening of European bloodlines. As the students filed out, my best student, a butch Dominican woman named Mia, muttered to me, "You're gonna get someone killed, man. This is *prison*." I waved goodbye to a couple of impassive guards on my way out through the yard.

When I arrived home at three o'clock, I got very stoned and drank whiskey and ice from a jumbo plastic cup. When Julia came home at six, I was a charming blend of catatonia and sentiment. I crooned about how I loved her while she encouraged me to shower. Once I did that, she wouldn't shut up about me putting on clothes, like there was some big rush. Apparently we were half an hour late for dinner. My carefully selected outfit proved compromised by obvious stains and missing buttons, so I changed and stumbled out the door in whatever, wrinkled jeans and a campfire-reeking lumberjack fleece with nothing under it. Julia drove.

"I'm glad to see you're feeling better," she said.

"What oh what will we *eat*?" I said. "You never know what they'll have! That's the thing about this place, you *never know*."

She paused, and made the surprising choice not to scream at me. *I* would have screamed at me.

"I got a poem accepted today," she said. "By a good place."

"Holy shit!" I yelled. "That's amazing! Where?"

She named the place. I yelled some more.

"It's really good for me," she continued calmly.

"Damn right!" I said. "*Now* we've got something to celebrate."

"Right, you can finally break your abstemious vigil."

"Shake 'em bake 'em absteamium sigil!" I said.

I cranked up the college radio station, which was playing a harpsichord song from the Renaissance or something, and waved my arms around like it was a party jam in a prom limo. Julia switched it to the actual hits station, which was playing Taylor Swift, and we sang along to her song about Starbucks. By the time we parked, I was better spirited and a little closer to sober.

"Oh, I hope they have that squid thing," Julia said, finally getting into it. "With the sauce?"

"They fucking better," I said.

This restaurant's defining design feature was that it had many more seats outside than inside, the tables sprawled across a wide patch of concrete and corralled by a severe metal fence. I spotted Leslie at a table right in the middle of the cluster, sitting next to a benign-looking fellow with a beard. I pointed them out to Julia and we floated over. I felt like I was walking too close to the other diners, like I was practically running my fingers through their food, though they didn't seem to notice. Leslie and her man stood when we reached them.

"Guys, this is Brian," she said. I looked him in the eye and shook his hand.

"Peter," I said. "Great to finally encounter you."

"Same, man," he said. He was a little pudgier than I expected him to be—pudgier than me, thank god—but he had the reedy, mellow voice of a smaller guy. "I've heard you guys are the picks of the litter."

"You shouldn't pick at litter," I said. "Gets you sick. She's a doctor."

"I can take care of any medical situations you may experience," Julia said. "Jockey bump, fox itch. Uh, metaplasmatosis."

"Great," he said uncertainly.

We sat down, and Julia apologized for our being so late.

"No worries," Leslie said. "We're still trying to catch up anyway."

"We were busy celebrating Julia's big publication news," I said. "We're going to need some cocktails very quickly."

"I just got a random poem accepted," Julia said. "It's not that big a deal."

"A doctor *and* a poet, huh?" Brian said. "That's *awesome.* Do you write poems about, like, your experiences as a doctor?"

"Sure, sometimes!" Julia said brightly. "I hear you write some, too? About food?"

"When I have time," Brian said. "Which isn't that much right now, unfortunately. It sucks when real life gets in the way."

"Got to avoid life," I said.

"Having money helps, doesn't it?" Leslie said. She was referring to the fact that I was a spoiled child. She studied my face, sending a message.

I ordered martinis from Kelly, a waitress three years out of the local MFA program. She wrote short stories about girls turning into butterflies, boyfriends revealed as Draculas, sea otters with charisma.

"Do you have that squid thing?" I said.

"Um, there's an octopus dish on the menu," she said. "Why don't you look at the menu while I get your drinks."

Her hostility was acceptable because, I remembered in that instant, she'd overheard me talking shit about her at a reading last year.

"We marked a couple of things on the menu that looked good, but we're easy," Brian said. "This place looks really great."

The menus were little pieces of paper, checklist-style, designed to get you to order a hundred small plates for fear of missing out. Everything sounded good, but the secret was that a quarter of the things were just steamed vegetables with some salt on them. I tried to look at my scrap of menu but it was dark and my vision is terrible, plus I didn't have the attention span right then. I pushed mine over to Julia and she neatly placed it under hers in understanding.

"Does everyone eat everything?" Julia said.

"I'm not super big on red meat," Brian said.

"Well, unless it's locally sourced, right?" Leslie said.

"I wasn't going to *say* that," Brian said. "The new people don't need to know what a weenie I am."

"They're not new to me, darling," Leslie said.

She was pointedly not looking in my direction.

Our drinks arrived, and Kelly gathered up the scribbled-on menus.

"Wait, did you guys finish figuring out what you wanted?" I said.

Leslie looked confused, Kelly exasperated.

"Whatever comes, we'll eat it," Julia said.

"Well, cheers," I said when the waitress had walked away. "To everybody being in the same place."

We all banged glasses, and no one commented on the paltriness of the stated occasion.

"Well, so how's your local food hub?" I said. "Isn't that where you work?"

"Ah, you know," Brian said. "You do your best. Nonlocal is always cheaper, and people like it better, because it's full of delicious chemicals, right? You kind of start to wonder how much it matters when the FDA keeps being like, it's fine, everyone. Enjoy the chemicals. You're all going to die from an opioid overdose anyway."

"That's the most pessimistic thing I've ever heard you say," Leslie said.

He shrugged and took a sip of his beer.

"Might need to get out of Texas," he said.

There was a pause as Julia and I searched for a way to continue that line of thought without stepping in it re: their plans for marriage, and therefore joint resettlement, or possible forfeit thereof by one particular party.

"Have you been getting stuff done out here?" Julia said to Leslie. "Any interesting adventures since the King of Pop torture party?"

"Been writing a little bit," Leslie said, betraying nothing. "*Reading* a lot, actually. Finished that Cormac McCarthy I stole from you guys—side note, maybe he's actually terrible?—and now on to James Welch. He's a big deal in Missoula. I love his first two books, but this one's harder to get into."

"I want to read *The Executioner's Song*," Julia said. "Peter won't stop talking about it."

"Oh, yeah," Leslie said. "I've read, um, parts of it. Really need to give it a full chance."

"It's worth it," I said.

"Has anyone here read the book about the hawk?" said Brian. "I hear that's amazing."

"T. H. White already did it," Julia said.

"I think it's kind of *about* T. H. White," Brian said.

"So why bother?" Julia said, more pointed now. "It seems like everybody wants to make me read and see shit that's just a lamer version of something that already exists. Like, why do I need to go see a movie where people pretend to be N.W.A. when I can just watch 'Fuck tha Police' on YouTube?"

"I like to see how things get interpreted," Brian said, really thinking it through. "You want to know what the contemporary take is, to be part of the conversation."

"That's what Peter says when he wants to watch the Oscars," Julia said. "But it's like, if everybody just rejected this shit, there wouldn't have to *be* a conversation. The conversation is *us*, you know?"

"Well, is it better to be solipsistic?" Leslie said. "Like, my friend Edward refuses to read any newspaper articles about the kids who do mass shootings, because he doesn't want to give them the attention. And it's like, dude, they're not going to stop covering shit people want to read about just because *you* don't want to read about it."

"But if everybody decided to stop, then it *would* make a difference," Julia said. "Like voting."

"It's *exactly* like voting," Leslie said. "It's a completely irrational activity. If *you*, Julia, decided to not pay any attention to who was running for president, and didn't vote ever again in your life, it would make not one whit of difference. Period."

"If *I* did that, it would signal some drastic shift in generational priorities, and it would be reflective of a changed culture. Similar to if everyone stopped reading about mass shooters."

"Right, but it wouldn't have *effected* the change. *That's* the difference."

Leslie had a pugilistic squint I hadn't registered before, a desire to curb stomp Julia on intellectual grounds. The debate had ceased to have any basis in concrete reality, but there was a sense of there being something real in the balance, a way of seeing the world vindicated or proven insufficient. (This was, of course, over a year before we found ourselves being teargassed with some regularity on something less than intellectual grounds. It doesn't get more concrete than pavement.)

"All I'm saying," Julia said with finality, "is that *I'd* rather take an active choice in the way I consume shit. That, for me, is a way of *feeling* less co-opted, even if it's basically a delusion. If I can ignore certain things, they can basically cease to exist."

"I mean, for sure," Leslie said.

Our first batch of food arrived shortly thereafter, three tiny plates of scattered leavings. Luckily we'd ordered a million more things. I got another drink and thought almost exclusively about

Brian fucking Leslie, the details of the act itself and also the bar-
barity of it in principle. The third time Brian complained about
Texas, I said, "Why don't you move *here*, man, or *somewhere*."

Leslie gave me the ghost of a scowl and I put my attention
on Brian, who was staring down at his mushrooms, or whatever
he'd scooped lately.

"We'll see," he said deliberately. "Everything's a little up in
the air at the moment, location-wise."

"It's not like I'm planning to stay here, anyway," Leslie said.
"It's just my little country retreat."

"Yeah, moving forward's the hard part," Julia muttered.

"I like the South," Brian said. "The music, the *attitude*. There's
some farms. I don't mind that it's a little slow."

"I'm just not a big-fish-small-pond kind of person," I said.
"I prefer to be ravaged by stimuli."

"How much have you had to drink?" Leslie said.

"As much as necessary," I said. "To get through this. I mean,
to get through this . . . life. Baby."

I felt a charge of recognition from Julia, the way she immediately put some food in her mouth instead of laughing or chid-
ing me.

The food finally stopped coming and Kelly brought us a
check, unbidden.

"Do you care about basketball?" I said to Brian. There was
an important West Coast playoff game that night.

"Yeah, I've been checking my phone to see if the game
started," he said. "Pretty invested in Steph Curry, like everybody."

"Well, shit," I said. "You wanna watch it at a bar or something?"

He looked at Leslie like a child up past his bedtime, as I'd
hoped he would. I actually did want to watch the game, but I also
wanted to delay, and possibly prevent, him from having a good
night with Leslie. I was willing to put myself in the way of his

company in order to take her out of it. Sacrifice: it's what Americans think love is.

"Do what you'd like," Leslie said in a good approximation of neutrality. "I'll take a bath, get some writing done. Unless you want to do something, Julia? Or do you want to watch the game, too?"

"I turn into a pumpkin pretty soon," Julia said. "And I really don't care about basketball. Even less than I care about the other ones."

"Me neither," Leslie said. "But wait, shit, how are we going to do the cars?"

I'd thought about this.

"You could drop Julia off on your way home?" I said. "And I'll drive Brian back to your aunt's place when we're done?"

"Do you know where it is?" Leslie said. The most explicit lie yet.

"GPS," I said.

"Are you going to be okay to drive?" Brian said.

"I will taper off," I said. "In three hours, it will be as though I'd never drank."

"He'll be okay," Julia said. "I know it's fucked-up, but he's a pretty good drunk driver."

"She's a doctor," I said.

"*Oh*-kay," Leslie said. "I'll leave you boys to measure Steph Curry's dick in peace."

"Spoiler alert: it's huge," I said.

Julia paid our half of the bill with her credit card, and I handed her a crumpled mess of ones and fives from my pocket. I couldn't see what she was leaving as a tip, possibly because she was intentionally shielding the receipt from me. I looked up and found Leslie's eyes fixed on me as Brian did something on his phone. She seemed very sad. It probably wasn't great that I was essentially forcing her and Julia to share a car. When Leslie sensed

Brian's attention returning, she broke eye contact with me and smiled blandly in his direction. The fact that I felt fully superior to him didn't do as much as I would have liked to quiet the panic rising continuously in me. My body was sure it was losing her, and it demanded booze in compensation.

"*Please* be good," Julia said when we got up to leave.

"You too," I said.

"I really don't feel like visiting the jail or the hospital tonight."

"Hey, me neither," I said. "I'll be foisting myself on you in the dark before you know it."

"Foisting yourself on the couch is more like it."

"Good *nigh*-ight," Leslie said, waving and opening the front door of her car. "Take care of my boy. He's not built for too much poison."

"I do what I want, woman," Brian said in a terrible imitation of a black speaking voice that had more of an edge to it than I would have expected.

I have a pretty clear memory of most of that night, but even while it was happening, it was like a dream, where you do things you don't want to do but can't control your own actions. Calmly, righteously, I drained double whiskeys on the rocks while lecturing Brian about James Harden and the ugly splendor of the Rockets' approach to basketball. I explained that by exploiting the foul rules, the Rockets had lifted the rock on the unseemly subjectivity of the contemporary NBA, something I'd read on the Internet recently. Brian didn't contribute much to the sports chat—it quickly became apparent that he was a recent joiner of the Golden State bandwagon, and also that he was mostly just with me to avoid spending time with Leslie. He also wasn't drinking much, the miserable fuck. If I had to watch televised sports without booze I'd kill myself out of boredom during the third Bud Light commercial.

And so with an inexplicably clear head and a stomach churning with tiny meals and bourbon, I asked him, in my best imitation of a man in a baseball cap, how things were with his girl.

"Like you don't know," he said.

"I've heard glimmers," I said. "Soundings."

"Well, she doesn't like me," Brian said, not whining. "I've

kind of looked down every hallway of this thing, and there's maybe just not that much more to it. I don't think she enjoys being *around* me anymore."

"You do something?" I said. "Tell the truth."

"I think about it all the time, and I've come up with a couple of things. I clogged the toilet a couple of months ago and had to go to work before I could fix it. That was bad. I waited until the last minute for her birthday and bought her this really expensive and ugly necklace that I knew she wouldn't like. She wears it all the time, to fuck with me I think. God, it's so ugly. There's more stuff like that."

"From what I can tell," I said, "Leslie is one of those people who needs to be honest with herself. Like, the self-deception, even when it happens, is pretty close to the surface."

"You're either describing yourself or you've been thinking about this a lot," Brian said. Not a complete moron, whatever his obvious downsides.

"Or talking out of my ass," I said, and theatrically drained my drink. "Can I buy you something?"

"I'm good," he said. "I've got the feeling I'm going to be driving you home."

"I'm walking," I said. I fished my car key out of my pocket, along with some receipts and more crumpled money. I spun the key toward him on the bar.

"Well, when the time comes, I'll drop you off," he said. He put the key in his pocket.

"I'm a man fancies a stroll come closing time," I said. "'Twas and 'twill be ever so."

"Sure," he said skeptically.

"Me and Julia, we're *really* good," I said. "Maybe you should follow our lead. We do this thing where we lean into our socially assigned gender roles in a really graphic way. That's how we maintain equilibrium in the modern world. Like, I'll come home, for one example, and she'll be naked in an apron baking cookies, and I'll lick all of the cookie dough off of her fingers while she mixes us martinis."

"Wait, what are you talking about?" Brian said.

"Yeah, I'll just be like, this house is a fucking *mess*, and the next thing I know she's on her knees scrubbing and breathing in all this supertoxic shit, and I'm outside building a tree house for the kid we don't have and burning like *hundreds* of fucking leaves on the barbecue grill. And then when the sun starts setting, she comes out with all these cookies and martinis and we just have sex in the yard and get bit to shit by mosquitoes while the hamburgers cook, with the neighbors and their dogs just like waving at us and smiling the whole time."

"Right."

"I'm saying that's what a successful relationship looks like. It's got to be super fucked-up and private. Shit you wouldn't tell anybody because they'd never understand. That's the only way it works."

He shook his head and smiled, eyes on the dull, waning basketball game. He'd decided to be amused.

"I think, actually, that a more conventional metric might apply here," Brian said. "Basic chemistry, life goals. I just want her to be happy. But I don't think that's what she wants."

"What does she want, do you think."

"Exactly," Brian said. "Exactly."

I signaled extravagantly for another drink, like a person drowning. The bartender, the big dude with blond heavy-metal hair and a despairing Nordic face, looked me in the eye and ignored me.

"Leslie is a beautiful person," I ventured. "She . . . well, *you*, I guess. *You* should do whatever it takes to make it work."

"You don't get it," Brian said. "I mean, I don't expect you to. It's just really hard when you've got something, and you think something is going to happen next, and then it's taken away from you. It's one thing when you don't know what you're losing, but to have it, and understand how precious it is, and still lose it . . . It fucking sucks."

The bartender warily set another drink down in front of me. A single, but still.

"I've had breakups," I said.

"I'm sure."

This would have been the perfect moment to reveal that I was having sex with his fiancée, and frequently, but I wasn't a killer like that. It wasn't my job. I mostly felt sad, sad for us, and for Julia and Leslie.

We sat in silence, staring at the TV screen. The moment I finished my drink—he had good peripheral vision, I guess, and decent manners—Brian gave a fake yawn and said, "I should really get back to Les, figure this shit out." My company had proved even less hospitable than hers.

"Gonna finish the game," I said, though it had long ceased to be competitive.

"Do you seriously want me to take your car?" Brian said. "How are you going to get it back?"

I flapped my wrist dismissively.

"Les can drive it into town sometime, or I'll go out there with Julia. My coche es tu coche. My phone is my shepherd, I shall not want."

"Okay, man," Brian said. He left a twenty on the bar, over-paying, and dismounted his stool. "This was fun. Hope it happens again."

"Remember what I told you," I said. "Outmoded gender roles, plus exhibitionist sex."

"Get home safe," he said. He clapped me on the shoulder, a little harder than necessary, and walked out.

"That was my stepdad," I said to the bartender. "Fucking bastard."

"We're closing up soon," he said.

"Game's still got like eight minutes left."

"C'mon, man," the bartender said. "Drink some water and go home."

He was a guy I usually liked, always decent to me. He'd told me the last time I was there that his wife had just had a baby daughter, their first, and I imagined he wanted to get home to them.

"Did you ever have the problem where you don't want to go where you're supposed to be, but you can't go where you want to be?" I said.

"Man, seriously, I don't know how you think you've earned any bartender advice," he said. "Go home to your wife, or girl-friend, or boyfriend, and try to be as quiet as you can getting into bed. Then you can talk about your stupid feelings in the morning."

"Was that so hard?" I said.

There was nobody on the street outside, and I didn't want to go home, which was at least a half hour away if I walked straight there. My phone was nearly dead, but I checked the progress of the basketball game repeatedly on it until it succumbed fully. That was what I wanted: some goddamn quiet.

Okay, my earlier claim of consistent clarity was a lie—the drinks always kick in when you least expect them to, and in this case it was in the fairly crucial period of remembering which way I needed to walk to get home. Mind you, this is a small city that I'd lived in for two years. If I know me, my thought process was that I'd take "the long way," which meant taking a bunch of turns through neighborhoods I didn't know. I probably realized I had no idea where I was, and followed the sounds of cars until I reached the highway, which I at least recognized. I have flashes of interaction preserved—being honked at by cars as I wandered along the shoulder of the road, being asked if I needed help by a homeless couple camped out by the trees—but when I came to full awareness a few hours later, there were traces of light in the sky, and I was on a quiet hilly road that I vaguely recognized, but didn't know which way I was walking on it. I trudged up a hill and realized how much my legs hurt. There was, in what looked like the near distance, a man sitting in a truck with the light on along the side of the road. After what felt like a day and a half, I reached him and looked in the window. He was masturbating to a picture of a large-breasted black woman in what appeared to be a vintage pornographic magazine. He looked up and saw me, pure terror in his eyes.

"Can you give me a ride into town?" I yelled.

"I am calling the police!" he yelled back, or something to that effect, from behind the window. He kept staring at me, fright and embarrassment shining in his dark eyes. "I am calling the police right now." He didn't move. Then he turned off the light in the cab. I stood there for another few seconds, then kept walking.

I'd gotten sober enough to realize I was in a bad situation. I wasn't going to die or anything, but I was at least a few miles from the house, with a dead phone, and Julia was going to be very unhappy with me. I suspected that I was walking in the wrong direction, but I did not have the fortitude to walk back in the direction from which I'd come. I mostly wished I could disappear, or wake up, but it turned out this was something that was actually happening.

With the sky brightening to dawn, I saw a silver Camry (that's what all midsize cars are to me, I guess) heading in the direction I thought I needed to go. I stuck my thumb out, standing nearly in the middle of the road, and he stopped.

"I'm really sorry," I said, "Can you take me into town by any chance?"

"You having some trouble?" he said.

"I walked farther than I meant to," I said. "Got kind of turned around."

"Don't shit a shitter, man."

"I may also have been slightly overserved."

"Get in if you don't mind hearing some about our Lord and Savior."

He talked about Jesus while I tried not to fall asleep in relief. We really weren't very far from town, and we were on a road that I'd driven many times before. He insisted on taking me to my front door, and would not accept the money I tried to hand him.

"Just think of this as God talking to you," he said. "I've been where you're at. You've got to let that stuff go. Look at this, you've got a nice house, dog in the window there. You want to lose all this?"

"I don't know," I said.

"Well, God knows that's not what you really want. He wants you to love Him, and love yourself. Yeah, I know, you don't want to listen to this rednecks-for-Jesus stuff. I forgive you."

"Thank you," I said. "I'll pass it on."

"Do what it takes to get right," he said. "Start with God."

When he drove away, I realized that Julia's car wasn't in front of the house, which was a very bad sign. Kiki was less affectionate than usual when I walked in, cringing away from my hand like I was a stranger. I plugged my phone in, waited for the battery picture to say "5%," and turned it on. I had a panicked voicemail from Julia, asking where I was, then a second one, in which she was in tears, pleading with me to call her back. Then I had one from Leslie. She sounded pissed. "Where are you, dude? Julia's freaking out. Whatever you're doing, it's not cool. Call me and tell me you're alive, please." I called Julia. "Where the *fuck* are you?" she said, on the verge of tears. "Home," I said. I hung up before she could respond. I turned off my phone again, and crawled into bed to wait for her return.

——•——

I waited a week, until I was reasonably sure Brian was gone, to email Leslie:

"Hey," I wrote,

> hope you had a good time with your out-of-towner. I hope I didn't cause too much trouble with him, or with anything else, due to my bad behavior. I think you understand, so I won't overexplain myself, but getting so drunk and ridiculous really was just an accident, one that I'm pretty embarrassed about. Would really love to see you, but understand if you'd rather not for whatever reason. Either way, be in touch.
>
> > Truly etc,
> > etc.

She didn't respond for twenty-four hours, which freaked me out, but when she did, I understood the delay.

"Hey," she wrote.

> Resurrection update: Brian and I are officially done. It was an ugly scene, and I ended up telling him I was seeing someone else to get it to finally stop, but don't worry, I didn't out you specifically. The one upside to you acting like such an idiot the other night is that he probably wouldn't suspect I'm involved with somebody who's such a mess. I hope Julia isn't too pissed at you. I

have the feeling she'll get over it, if she's gotten over dealing with you in general.

Just to be clear, I certainly didn't leave Brian "for you" or anything like that, and I've gotten the impression that you're relatively happy with Julia, despite our whatever. I really don't want to be the person that fucked up your life. Anyway, you want to get together and chat some of this out? Not that it needs to be a super heavy conversation. But it would be good to know where we're at.

Yrs,

L.

Molly, majestic in her amorality, agreed to let Leslie and me meet up at her house on a night when she was planning to stay over with Gil, with whom she was "spending time" again.

"No sex in my bed, though," she said over the phone. "Seriously. That's my one rule."

"That's not what this is," I said. "You have nothing to fear."

"You can have sex literally anywhere else," she said. "I just really really don't like other people in my bed without me present."

I brought half a bottle of bourbon, not clear on the plan. Julia had her writing group that night, a loose coalition of local poets and memoirists across a wide age range that met every month to read their latest work and offer supportive criticism. It gave her a reason to finish things. Plus there was usually dessert.

When I got to Molly's, Leslie's car was already parked out front. I found her in the kitchen, slouched over the counter drinking a beer and reading a big, splayed-open hardcover.

"There's the man," she said.

"Hey there," I said.

I moved toward her, planning on a stiff, awkward embrace, but she leaned into it, pulled me toward herself tightly.

"I feel like such a *shit*," she said, her chin heavy on my shoulder.

"About Brian?" I said.

"Just everything," she said.

She stepped back and looked me over appraisingly.

"You look skinny," she said.

"Yeah, right," I said. "It's really good to see you."

"I know," she said. "Do you have any, uh, Salinger on you?"

I fished the vaporizer out of my pocket and gave it to her. She took a pull from it and contemplated the ceiling.

"The Brian thing . . ." she said, gathering her thoughts. "I pretty much knew at first sight. That it wasn't going to happen, I mean. But I felt like I couldn't just tell him to turn around, you know? I guess that might've been the adult thing to do. He's really mad at me, which is fair. At least he got a little more sex out of it? Though I feel pretty ambivalent about that, too. It's probably the most I've ever felt like an actual whore. Just, like, fucking somebody because I felt like it was my *job*. Not a lot of fun, I have to say."

I felt light-headed, and unreasonably hurt.

"Did you . . . come?" I said.

"What?" she said. "I mean . . . yeah. I did. Is that not allowed? It was still *pleasurable*. Physically. Just not ideal."

"Sorry, that was a kind of fucked-up thing to ask," I said.

"I mean, I don't ask you about what you and Julia do."

"It's not that interesting."

"Of *course* it is. It's just that I'd rather not know about it. I realize I can seem kind of glib about this shit, but I'm very capable of being hurt by it, too. I don't want you to think that's not the case."

"I get it," I said. "What do you want me to do?"

She raised her eyebrows as she took a long sip of beer.

"What I want and what's possible aren't necessarily compatible."

She fixed me with her eyes. I felt myself vulnerable to her in a way that was different from Julia. In Leslie's presence, I felt a constant calling to be different from myself, not better, but *more*, to rack my brain for a more interesting thing to say, to find some new way to please.

"I want to be whatever you want me to be," I said deliberately. "I can live with whatever that is."

I hadn't expected to say that, and now that I had, I wondered if it was true. It sounded true.

"That's . . . well, that's good to know," Leslie said.

The thrill of submission was heady. Better than the booze. Or, good mixed with the booze.

"I don't even *like* most people," she said, exasperated. "And here I am wasting all my time with you. But I want you to be sure about things. You're not actually sure unless you're sure. Like, you can't be just a little bit pregnant."

"You're not pregnant, right?" I said. I smiled like a monkey.

"Christ, I sure fucking hope not. No offense to either of you."

"So . . . what now, then?"

"Well," she said.

"Molly said to stay out of her bed," I said.

"Don't have a peasant mentality," Leslie said.

We fucked on the couch, more abruptly and desperately than usual, mostly clothed. There was something different in how we treated each other now. When you first have sex with someone, especially when they're otherwise committed, there's both a performativity and a withholding, a contradictory set of impulses to demonstrate one's value as a performer and to not commit fully to the emotional experience commensurate with great sex, lest your feelings prove an embarrassment. That night at Molly's, Leslie and I got past compatibility, to that place where you surprise yourself with how badly you want to stay in that liminal pocket together, how desperate and unattractive you're willing to be to experience uncompromised joy.

When we were finished, we lay on our backs on the rough rug.

"Well, okay," Leslie said. "Fine."

Part IV

L eslie met Brian in the middle of her second year in Missoula. She'd gotten through a master's in art history without learning very much, but she'd enjoyed the classes, and despite some predictable instances of backsliding, she was sober significantly more frequently than not. She was surprised at how good she felt about this.

Kim, her closest friend in town, had been a graduate student in the writing program years before and decided to stay on in Missoula, working in the bookstore and writing her endlessly proliferating memoir. Kim didn't necessarily believe that she ever had to finish her book. She was interested, conceptually, in the notion of an infinitely expanding text, one that continued to accrue material. She recognized that this was not a new concept; it was, she said, a distinctly modernist impulse. Modernism, Kim said, still hadn't quite found its way to the Mountain West, and it was better that it arrive late than never. Leslie wasn't entirely convinced that modernism needed to land in the West at all. What would it do there? Like, for fun?

Kim had introduced Leslie to her people, former writing students and artists and beer connoisseurs of varying degrees of talent and ambition. The only keeper from Leslie's art history program was a married sometime-cowboy in his early thirties named Mason who was getting his degree as research for his "purely mercenary" *Da Vinci Code* rip-off. This was proving harder to write than he'd initially imagined it would be. Mason drank a lot. "It's the *principle!*" he would say, often without a clear referent.

One night, Leslie went to the Steel Pony, the terrible, over-priced sports bar, to keep Kim spiritual company for an hour or two of her shift. It was not a place in which she, or any of her friends, willingly spent time, though one sometimes ended up there at the end of a night, always with, or at the behest of, men.

Leslie was sitting at the bar alone reading Annie Dillard while sports and replays of sports screamed all around her. She didn't understand why people would choose to drink here when Missoula had so many grimier, cheaper bars in which to get drunk. It hadn't yet occurred to her that people might grow tired of spending their time in cheap, grimy bars.

"Oh, what do you think of that?"

It came from a guy two stools over from her. His question was better than the usual—"Is that a book?" or "Reading in a bar!" or, once, in this very place, simply "Boooooo!" She checked him out. A little scruffy, a little pudgy, baseball cap, green zip-up hoodie.

"It's great," she said. "Have you read her?"

"I'm a big fan of *Tinker at Pilgrim Creek* or whatever it's called, but it's the only one I've read. Is that an essay collection?"

"Yeah. She makes a big deal about how it's not *just* an essay collection, though. I mean, I *love* a random-shit assemblage, but I guess she wants to make sure we know it's *seriously considered*."

"Huh," the guy said. "Cool. I'm Brian, by the way. Sorry for interrupting. I know how annoying it is, but I couldn't resist."

"No worries," Leslie said, words she hated to hear coming

out of anyone's mouth, especially her own. "Leslie. I'm just keeping my friend who works here company."

"Not your scene?" Brian said lightly.

"I'm not judging," Leslie said. "I wish I cared about sports, honestly. It'd make the twenty-first century a little more comfortable."

"They hook us young," Brian said. "This is the only place with enough TVs to waste one on my terrible baseball team." He gestured to one of the eight televisions over the bar.

"You're a fan of . . . LAD?"

"Twins," he said.

"That's a good one," Leslie said. "That's, like, even less threatening than any of the bird ones."

"Well, they could be really tough twins. Or twin dragons or something."

"Word, good point. Are you here by yourself?"

"Waiting on a friend."

"Ah. Girl."

"Friend. Friend girl. Work friend girl."

"Get that distance, boy."

"Yeah, I just like to be clear."

"What do you and friend girl do? For work?"

"We're part of this organic food nonprofit. Green Apple? We're trying to get good food to underserved communities. Low-income people, reservations. You'd think it'd be an easy sell out here, but once you get out of Missoula, it gets harder."

"Hostile?" Leslie said.

"More indifferent. I do get it. I'm not somebody who thinks everyone needs to be eating all organic food. We're just trying to make sure people have access if they want it."

"No need to be defensive," Leslie said. There was a carefulness to his demeanor that had the potential to be interesting, if it wasn't just cowardice.

His eyes went over her head to the door, where a squat woman with bangs was waving in his direction.

"Leslie, this is Mariah," Brian said. "We literally just met," he said to Mariah.

"That's cool," Mariah said, her tone implying the opposite. "How're your boys doing?"

"Ummmmmm . . ." He looked up at the screen. "Losing! Not a surprise."

Leslie could feel the psychic tremors of barely concealed annoyance radiating from Mariah. Brian had come here to watch the game, not flirt with some large-handed slut. She either was more than a work friend or hoped to be.

"Brian was telling me about what you guys do," Leslie said. "It sounds like really important stuff."

"It is and it isn't," Mariah said, her voice a sigh. "There's always some more significant thing you could be doing, right?"

"Mariah's a native," Brian said. "Hellgate High, UM, the whole package."

"I fucking *love* Hellgate," Leslie said. "I don't think the kids appreciate how badass it is that that's the name of their high school."

"I mean, it's kind of like, who are you going to tell?" Mariah said. "Wherever you go to high school is going to suck."

"Yeah, I guess I went to prep school," Leslie said, and stopped. "Anyway, I don't want to interrupt your guys' thing here. It was nice to meet y'all."

"Oh!" Brian said. "I mean, you don't have to *go*."

Leslie smiled, self-consciously turning on the charm.

"I know I don't *have* to," she said.

"Stick around for one more drink," Brian said. "I never meet anybody."

"Let me buy you guys a round, at least," Leslie said. "What do you want, Mariah?"

"Whatever you're having," she said.

So the night at the Steel Pony continued, Mariah's intransigence no match for Brian's interest. She and Brian finally ditched her when they declared their interest in migrating to the Rose—big surprise, Mariah couldn't *stand* the place, probably because it was awful. But Leslie felt safe there, in the irradiated light, among the scruffy drunks and the not-scruffy-enough students. It was carpeted, attached to a casino, too dark in the front and too bright by the bar. The décor was not random chic, just ill-considered: an amateur painting of a mountain landscape, a taxidermied antelope head, a poster of the painting of Kramer from *Seinfeld*, a framed photograph of the Ali-Frazier knockout. Even the TVs didn't know what to do—they were usually tuned to whatever movie was on TNT, or the news. At six o'clock, she'd learned from drinking through some windy weekday afternoon, the regulars played along with *Jeopardy!*

She sipped her whiskey at the table in the front window, the one that glowed seriously pink, knowing that there was no way she looked sexy in this light and happy about it. She'd gotten into a mood of debasement, despite the earlier awakening of something like her higher self. She knew it was mostly the booze, and that it would be good not to go janky on this guy.

"You," Brian said. He paused and took a pull of his beer. "You know, there are not many awesome people."

"Aw," Leslie said. "Come now. Look around you." The bar was amusingly bereft of even potentially awesome people. "But I mean. I try."

"I think I try too hard, maybe," Brian said. "I feel like every time I find out about something it's kind of lost its glow. I don't know how you get *ahead* of the curve, rather than just *on* it."

"You gotta forget about the curve," Leslie said. "Giving up is the only path. Like Buddhism."

"Oh, are you into Buddhism?"

"Naw," she said. "Just talkin'."

He nodded with unnecessary seriousness.

"I meditate pretty frequently, I guess," he said. "It really helped with stress, which helped with the migraines. It's obvious, but so much stuff really *is* mental, if not, you know, spiritual or whatever. People get super goofy about it, but just, like, *acknowledging* the benefit of mindfulness, or whatever you want to call it, has done good things for me. It's like, if it works it works. As William James didn't quite say."

"Did *not* expect to hear that name," Leslie said.

"Yeah, I'm kind of a whore for the history of psychology. That was what I did in undergrad. Really interesting, if fairly useless."

"I'm sold," Leslie said.

"What do you mean?" Brian said.

She nudged his hand across the table. He turned his palm over, thinking she wanted to hold his hand, but she instead kept pushing it toward his pint of beer.

"Finish your drink," she said.

———•———

Brian was slightly better in bed than she'd expected him to be, more assertive, considerate but not overly deferential, as she'd worried he might be. And this small exceeding of expectations proved to be a pattern. He knew about science and economics and politics, and he'd traveled around the world, especially in Asia, where Leslie had never been, or even seriously considered going.

They went to an Iranian film at the Wilma. It was in the tiny side theater while a concert was going on in the main hall, and they were the only ones in the audience. Leslie had been dying to see the movie—it had come out three months earlier in New York and was the favorite to win Best Foreign Film. Of course, it was dull as rocks. One of the child protagonists actually *collected* rocks. She usually loved boring movies, loved to sit and stare at people's big faces as they stared at other things, even when there was a second-tier jam band making supposedly joyful noise through the wall. But she was nervous about how Brian was taking it, and tried to read his expression obliquely, so as not to seem overly solicitous and draw a reassuring smile, or, worse, a grimace. But every time she glanced at him, his eyes were engaged, seemingly without affect, by what was happening on the screen, his mouth set in a slight frown of concentration. So maybe the movie *wasn't* boring. She decided to test him by putting her hand on his thigh and slowly pressing her fingers against his dick through his pants. He remained focused on the screen.

"Do you like that?" she whispered.

He smiled and jutted his chin at the screen.

"Arian's goldfish might not make it," he whispered.

She settled back into her seat.

When the movie was over, they walked up Higgins in the direction of the Union.

"Did you really like it?" Leslie said.

"I thought it was interesting," Brian said. "I wouldn't have thought to see it, you know?"

"But you're glad you did."

"I'm . . . yeah. You could say that."

"I thought it was kind of boring, honestly," Leslie said. "His other stuff is better."

"Oh!" Brian said, considering this. "Well. I guess I was trying not to think about it in terms of boring or not boring. It was like, this is the kind of thing this is, and it's definitely unfolding at, like, its own pace. I didn't really consider whether I was *bored* or not."

"Huh," Leslie said. She didn't know whether this was admirably open-minded or just kind of dumb. But over the next few months, she found herself drifting into something like happiness with Brian. She drank less—mostly beer, which wasn't great on a caloric level, obviously, but whatever—and cut down to two cigarettes a day, in large part because Brian couldn't stand the smell of them. He did, thank god, like weed, though, and they spent many sunny evenings on the deck of the new brewery, nursing a couple of beers for hours, reading and chatting and playing cards. They hiked in the Rattlesnake and cooked Indian food with Kim and watched the multipart television versions of *Fanny and Alexander* and, somewhat less wisely in a new relationship, *Scenes from a Marriage*. It was quite nice.

So she tried to destroy it. She went to a barbecue in her friend Sam's backyard on a Friday night, got blackout drunk, and, she was told later, made out with someone's girlfriend. She spent the night on Sam's couch, awoke too hungover to leave, took mushrooms with Sam, watched eight hours of a violent fantasy television series, had elaborate, cerebral sex with Sam inspired by the feelings evoked by said fantasy series, then slept until noon the next day, all the while ignoring calls, texts, and emails from Brian. Sam, to his credit, didn't inquire about her relationship status, and did not seem to take it amiss that she might spend a weekend doing his drugs and having sex with him without expecting anything further in the way of future romantic involvement. And this was good, because she woke to a Mumford & Sons station streaming tinnily from Pandora through his laptop speakers.

On Sunday evening she texted Brian, writing that she'd been out of town camping with no cell service (this despite the fact that she'd refused to go camping with him on numerous occasions because she "hated tents"), and asking if he wanted to hang out. She received no response. The silence persisted through the first half of the week. On Wednesday, she went to Bernice's, their usual café, in an attempt to stake him out.

The place was busy for a Wednesday afternoon. She ordered a large coffee and a cookie shaped like the state of Montana. She managed to snag a table right as an insane local artist was leaving it. Next to her, a child—maybe three years old?—with a gloriously untamed mop of dark hair bashed an action figure against the corner of an unvarnished wood table while his minders sat across from one another staring into their laptops.

She recognized the toy—it was a replica of a professional wrestler circa 1992. The Ultimate Warrior. Her older brother, Steven, had owned that one and dozens more, spending his mid–single digits smashing them into each other in the course of hermetic, byzantine narratives. She'd joined in occasionally—as older brothers went, he'd been on the sensitive side—but it was clear that it required great effort on his part to make the sharing of his private world comprehensible and fun. More frequently, they played with their gender-mandated human simulacra across the room from each other, she freely mixing Barbies and life-size baby dolls and miniature horses in swirling psychodramas with no clear narrative thrust. Whereas Steven's wrestlers seemed to follow a more or less filmic pattern of violent antagonism followed by grudging acceptance of one another to defeat some larger evil (often represented by faceless vehicles that dwarfed them in size, hence the teamwork), her women, babies, and animals simply bickered continually, never achieving resolution. The sources of their complaints were mostly lost to her now—surely a bricolage of overheard and misunderstood adult phrases coupled with vague rehashings of concerns gleaned from television—but she remembered her engrossment in them, the dreamy endlessness of the afternoons spent deep in her own mind.

The child perched his Ultimate Warrior on the rim of his

father's giant coffee mug, then plunged him in, sending coffee spilling down the sides of it and onto the table.

"Hey, hey!" the father said, as if surprised to find a child there at all. "That is *not* what we do!"

He fished the action figure out of his cup, set it down on the table, and went back to his computer.

Leslie stayed until closing time, waiting, thinking. Brian did not appear.

After a full week—he was apparently avoiding all of the town's bars and cafés, not an easy feat—her resolve broke and she called him. She left him a voicemail, straining to sound casual.

She went to his house on Saturday afternoon, the least aggressive time, she thought, to confront your pseudo-boyfriend unannounced. He answered the door warily, like he knew exactly who it would be. He was wearing a Griz sweatshirt and mesh shorts.

"Hey, Les," he said.

"Oh, 'hey,'" she said. She thought the quotation marks were clear. There were very few good language options available.

"What's up?" he said.

"Look, can we just get right to it?" she said. "I understand if you don't want to see me anymore, I guess, but I'd prefer to, like, take it on the chin."

"I'm not going to punch you," he said.

"Right, what a shame," she said. "Can I come in? Is what's-her-name hiding in there?"

He smirked in a way that twisted his usually placid face. It made him a little ugly.

"You're interrupting the grand orgy finale," he said. "The climax, if you will."

"Well shit, dude. You *know* I'm into strangers. Where's my invite?"

"Thought you might be camping again. Thought that was your new weekend hobby."

"Aw, man," she said. "I had an adventure, okay? I learned my lesson."

"I wasn't trying to teach you anything," Brian said. "I was just mad at you. Still am, actually."

"Okay," Leslie said. "So, what? You're some jealous dude and you don't want to see me anymore? That's it?"

"Yeah, that's the entirety of my character."

"Well, say what you fucking *mean*, man. If you want to be, whatever, *exclusive*, I'll reluctantly consider it. For you."

"I actually have to meet someone, like, now," he said. "Not your beloved Mariah. But, you know, someone. Let's figure something out soon."

He was trying to walk a hard line here, but Leslie saw the quiver in his mouth. He was not a hard person, which was one of the things that Leslie liked about him.

"So, that's not going to happen," she said. "What I'm going to do is, I'm going to come inside. And you're going to have about thirty seconds to cancel your plans, if you actually have plans, which I don't believe you do. That's your option."

He stared at the ground, and when his eyes reached hers again, he looked like he was about to cry.

"I was really trying to make a point," he said.

"I know," she said. "I know you were." She saw her moment— she stepped forward and wrapped him in a hug. He put his arms around her and let her rest her chin on his shoulder, but he didn't squeeze back.

"Can we go inside?" she said.

"Yeah, I guess," he said. "I'll tell my friend to meet us here."

"Is that really what you want to do?"

He took off his Twins cap and ran his hand through his flattened hair.

"I told Patrick I'd watch the Iowa game with him," he said. "Don't make me be an asshole to him, okay? Please?"

They watched the game, all three of them, and Leslie was almost relieved enough to enjoy it.

Part V

*T**his* was when the angst and dishonesty really kicked in. Now that it felt like there was a decision to make, any time I spent apart from Leslie took on a heightened urgency. I'd asked her why we couldn't spend time together at her aunt's house. The answer was that her aunt didn't work and was in and out of the house at unpredictable intervals. I reminded Leslie that she was nearly thirty years old, and she explained that her aunt was sternly moralistic in matters pertaining to sex and, additionally, would report the presence of a new partner to her mother. Apparently Leslie's mom was a big fan of Brian, and had gone from despondent to devastated as Leslie moved from unsure to firmly broken up with him. I'd spent enough time with Julia's folks to know that one underestimates family dynamics at one's peril.

I wasn't ready to become the kind of person who committed his infidelities in a motel, nor was I interested in further enlisting the help of friends who might resent my sleazy favor requests and/or bring their concerns to Julia. So I did something that you're not supposed to do, one more addition to an expanding universe of said things: I invited Leslie over to the house while Julia was at work.

We were spotted pulling up to the house by my neighbor Peggy, home on an apparent lunch break. Peggy's dog, Charleston (a "she," confusingly), played with Kiki a few days a week in her yard or ours, and most of the text messages I received between nine and five every day were from Peggy, asking if Kiki wanted to play with Charleston, wondering if I could bring the dogs in or put them out depending on the weather, asking for updates on Charleston's baroque health problems, which were often brought on by her tendency to binge eat anything within her range of vision. Peggy had been, at some point, born again in Christ's love, and though she didn't explicitly evangelize, she "accidentally" referred to Julia and me as husband and wife, and inevitably invited us to join her for church if she spotted us between Friday afternoon and Sunday morning, an invitation we always politely declined.

As Leslie and I got out of the car, Peggy came lurching toward us, tugged forward by Charleston, who was being urged on by Kiki's frantic flinging of herself against the front window of the house.

"It stopped raining, so I thought I'd bring Charlie over to play!" Peggy said. She gave Leslie a momentary glance and then turned back to me. "You're not teaching today?"

"The prison's on lockdown," I said, which was true.

"Oh," she said. She'd made it clear that she generally didn't approve of my teaching at the prison. Those women needed Christ, not composition. "Well, I don't want to interrupt if you have company." She looked at Leslie again, longer this time.

"No, it's fine," I said. "I'll just put them in the backyard."

"Why don't I put them in my yard?" she said. "That'll be easier for you while you're entertaining."

She clearly didn't want to leave her dog with potential fornicators. Kiki was attempting to kill herself against the window in excitement, and I worried that Charleston was going to rip Peggy's arm off.

"That's very sweet of you," I said. "I'll bring Kiki out for you. Leslie, this is Peggy. Leslie's a writer, Peggy. We're talking about collaborating on a screenplay."

Peggy brightened with obvious false cheer.

"How exciting!" she said. "You must be friends with Peter's wife, Julia, as well!"

"I am, yes," Leslie said, giving her a shit-eating grin in response. "She's really wonderful."

"I just love her," Peggy said.

I walked to the front door and let Kiki out. She nearly knocked Peggy over with joy, then cowered away from Leslie when she tried to pet her. Peggy's eyes gleamed in triumph.

"She takes some time to warm up," she said.

"I know," Leslie said stiffly. "I've been here before. A few times."

"Well, good luck with the writing!" Peggy said. "You can come get her whenever, Peter, or I'll bring her back when I get home."

"Thanks, I can do it," I said.

"Whatever's easiest for you," Peggy said, already being dragged back toward her house by Charleston, with Kiki running circles around both of them in joy.

"Sorry," I said when we got inside. "She means well. Or, I mean, the opposite."

"I wouldn't be surprised if she and my aunt go to Bible study together," Leslie said. "That's *exactly* what all of her friends are like."

I felt trapped in the small house, watched by passersby. We read on the couch together for a while like we did at Kenny's, she with her head in my lap, but we did too much shifting around to make any progress. After half an hour, she got up and stood in front of the biggest bookcase, then moved methodically to the one next to it, then cycled through each row of each of the six cases in the room.

"What are you looking for?" I said.

"Nothing in particular," she said.

"Are you sure?"

"What, do you think I'm *secretly* looking for something?"

"You just seem very deliberate," I said.

She sighed heavily and pulled something out, randomly or not, I couldn't tell, and started paging through it. I looked down at my book and tried to keep myself from glancing at her, even peripherally, and she seemed committed to doing the same with the book in her hands. I broke first, of course.

"What is that?"

"Lowell," she said, curt but not quite snapping.

He was Julia's favorite poet, and I tried to remember whether or not I'd told Leslie this. If not, it seemed slightly uncanny, though I suppose the number of his volumes in the house upped the odds. Plus, he was a lot of people's favorite poet.

She put the book back on the shelf and sat down next to me on the couch.

"I just wanted to check something," she said.

"Is there something I can do?" I said.

"I didn't feel like a creep before," she said. "Which was probably my own failing, I realize. But it's a real thing."

"Let's just go out for lunch," I said. "We're still just people. Friends, you know? Like, in real life."

"I don't want to go out for lunch," she said. "I want us to do our thing and not feel guilty about it."

"You're always going to feel guilty about something," I said.

"I don't think that's true. I hope it's not. What I don't like right now is how badly I want to get fucked-up just so I don't feel like a shitty person."

That *did* seem like a problem.

"Let's . . . what do people do?" I said. "I bet we have some food. Are you hungry?"

"Probably," she said. "I didn't eat anything today."

There was half a baguette on the kitchen counter, a bunch of cheese in various stages of decomposition in the fridge, some tomatoes and apples, a quarter tub of hummus. I made coffee and assembled a vaguely presentable smorgasbord (cohabitation comes with the occasional useful skill), and we ate sitting kitty-corner at the end of the moldier-than-usual dining room table. Through the window, the squirrels were asserting unspeakable privileges with Kiki away, foraging in the piles of decayed leaves and chasing each other around the huge tree in the corner of the yard. I watched Leslie transform as she chomped on loaded chunks of bread. Her eyes widened, gained hints of blue. She perched straighter in her chair and lightly pressed her fingers against my hand to emphasize a point she was making about how the biopic industrial complex was destroying America. Food! It turns out you need to eat food!

We were still a little shaky. We watched a couple of episodes of a surrealist sketch show on the Internet—during the day! the pinnacle of decadence!—which, despite its screaming and grotesquerie, eventually led to us making out on the couch like a married couple just home from a counseling breakthrough. She squirmed away from me, smiling, her skirt riding up to reveal almost parodically ugly beige underwear that hung loose off of her hips. When I moved my face toward her, she slapped me hard.

"No," she said, still smiling. She stayed in the same position, making no further move.

"Hmm," I said. I moved my hand tentatively toward her crotch, and she drew back her arm sharply, so I retreated. She nodded curtly at the erection visible beneath my black jeans. I

cautiously unbuckled my belt, unbuttoned my pants, and looked
to her for approval. Another curt nod. I pulled my jeans off. Nod.
Boxers. Nod. I reached my hand toward her again—a minute
headshake. I put my hand on my cock. Nod. Raised an eyebrow.
Nod. Indicated with my eyes that I was positioned fairly promi-
nently in front of an open window. Nod.

If it was to be done, I guessed it was best to be done quickly.
She remained still, watching me with attention as I moved my
hand over my cock. I raised my eyebrows again, to indicate that
things were getting serious. She looked down at my busy hand,
then back up into my eyes. I wasn't going to stop unless she told
me to. She didn't. So she got, I guess, what she wanted.

"Did that feel good?" she said.

"So it seems," I said. I tried to appear casual in my assessment of where the traces of my enthusiasm might have landed.
Mostly my shirt, it seemed. Cool.

"Was it as good as fucking me?"

"Is that a trick question?"

"It's more like a koan," she said.

I pondered this.

"Don't you want anything?" I said.

"Oh, no," she said. "It's *your* house."

We were going to have to find another place, was the elabo-
rately delivered message, apparently. Or, I could cease to *live* in
this house.

On the drive back to her aunt's, Leslie abruptly turned off
the bluegrass on the college radio station.

"I meant to tell you," she said. "Well, I deliberately chose not
to tell you, I guess. But now I'm telling you. There's a semester-
long teaching job open in Montana. They had somebody flake out
for the fall, and they can't pay shit, so they're kind of scrambling
for somebody to teach a couple of classes. Apparently I'm a quote
strong candidate for the job if I want it, probably because they

literally don't have anyone else. So I'm going to jump through the interview and syllabus hoops and whatever and see what happens. I just thought you might want to know."

"I mean, that's awesome, right?" I said.

"It's *something*," she said. "It's not nothing."

"Is there some universe in which you *don't* want to do it?"

"Well, it wasn't really the plan," she said.

"It's no central Virginia," I said.

"That would really solve your problem, wouldn't it?" she said. "A little tidy, but life goes on."

I pointedly ignored what she was getting at. "I've never been to Montana," I said. "I'm only vaguely aware of where it is. I guess it's basically Wyoming?"

"Maybe you'll tell Julia about all this someday. After she cheats on you. You've got an ace just waiting in the hole."

"If you get the gig, we'll see what happens."

"My point is, it's really not going to be your problem."

I was nearly shaking before the possibilities this opened, the gaping maw of the future suddenly present before me. I spent so much time on the daily logistics of just staying alive that I often went weeks without remembering that I had no idea what I was doing with my life. I knew, because I'd been told, that passivity was not a quality to aspire to. But I thought it was possible that there was some secret nobility, a logic, in letting the tides of life just knock one around, in keeping the psychic ledger balanced.

When I dropped Leslie off, neither of us made a move to kiss the other goodbye.

Julia had the next day off so we went hiking in Shenandoah with Kiki, a steep uphill trudge to a big-deal view that we'd seen a half dozen times. I imagined Montana, thought about how the mountains and views there were probably better in every sense, but then tried to figure out whether or not that actually mattered to me. So it was prettier, grander. It would still be standing on a mountain, looking at other mountains, right? You'd still have to come down. We ate peanut butter and banana sandwiches and almonds on our hike and tried to get Kiki to drink out of the portable fold-up dog bowl we'd wasted fifteen dollars on. You can lead a dog to water.

On the way back we stopped at the brewery-restaurant on the edge of the Blue Ridge. Kiki strained at her leash, trying to ambush a shivering Pekinese two tables over. This I would miss, this approximation of well-curated middle-class happiness. The late-afternoon sun paired with a citrus-infused IPA. Stupid stuff.

"You excited for Maine?" I said. We were supposed to go to Julia's parents' place in a week to celebrate her finishing another year of med school and me giving all of my summer prison students As.

"Actually, we need to talk about what's going on with you," Julia said.

I gave an exaggerated rictus smile.

"You are . . . depressed? Bored?"

"Are there other feelings?" I said.

"Right, the usual," she said. "So . . . what? Do you want to have sex with someone else? A different kind of sex? More? Less?"

She was trying to keep it light, but I could tell she was on the verge of tears. Had I been that out of it? I really couldn't remember whether she'd brought up anything like this lately. I'd thought she was going to ask if I was an alcoholic, though I suppose that would've been awkward over beers.

"I mean . . . I know I've been weird," I said. "I feel kind of burned-out."

"Burned-out from what?" Julia said.

"Just . . . being myself, I guess. I'm not saying I'm bored with anything other than myself."

"So you're depressed."

"Well, but I do feel better sometimes."

"When?"

Don't say drugs, don't say Leslie.

"When I can imagine things changing," I said, which was in the ballpark of the truth.

There was a long silence, though of course the people at the other tables kept screaming away.

"Between us?" Julia said, like she was clearing her throat.

"I don't know," I said. I took a long swallow of beer and felt it curdle in my mouth.

"Does this have anything to do with Leslie?" she said.

Somehow, I was shocked to hear her named. I looked just above Julia's eyes, right into the center of her forehead.

"Naw," I said. "She might be moving soon, actually."

Julia perked up, curled her lip at me.

"And how do you feel about that."

"Kind of bummed," I said. "I hope we stay in touch. If she goes."

"Have you had sex with her?" Julia said, wonderingly. "I guess it makes sense."

"Don't say that," I said.

"*Is* that true?"

"Of course not," I said. "There's some, you know, *tension* between us, though. For sure. We're both *attracted* to each other. In some ways. But that's not a crime, right?"

"Having *sex* with her isn't a crime, Peter. We're not talking about crime."

"Look," I said, shading male, reasonable. "I'm not going to pretend there's not something between us. I don't think it's anything you need to worry about. It's just an . . . understanding."

Julia shook her head slowly, looked me in the eye, looked away, looked back.

"*We* have an understanding," she said.

"Well, it's nice to have another one," I said.

"I'm not, you know, taking this lightly," Julia said. "If something *happened*, I think we can talk about it. But if you won't talk about it, I don't know. It's hard to know what to do with that."

"Would you countenance the possibility that there's nothing to talk about?"

"There's always something to talk about. That's basically your catchphrase. You've *berated* me for not having something to talk about."

"I meant, obviously, on this particular subject. I should have owned up to the, I don't know, *intensity* of our friendship. You're right. But that's all it is. You shouldn't push and push to see if I'm going to give."

"See, you keep taking it one step further, Pete. That's why I keep pressing."

"I'll do a better job of being present. My class is finished, and I'm going to have some time to work on my own stuff. I'm really looking forward to that."

"Right. It's not like ninety percent of your time isn't already available to you for whatever the fuck it is you get up to."

"We can't all be learning how to cure cancer and writing the great fucking unreadable poem of the century."

"I'm glad the blame lies squarely with *my* ambitions."

"Yeah, Jules, this is a real Rosie the Riveter moment."

"Fuck you! I don't think I've ever actually said that to you before. But seriously. Fuck. You. I'm not crazy."

"That's . . ."

"Enough," Julia said. "Finish your beer and let's go."

We didn't speak on the drive home, which felt twice as long as usual. I rummaged through my head for some aggrieved indignation but I couldn't summon it. I didn't feel as guilty as I should have—maybe the sudden narrowing of my options provided a kind of moral anesthetic. It didn't *matter* how I felt, which, I guess, didn't usually get in the way of feeling things. But there I was.

Julia and I started the drive to Maine on a Friday morning, with Kiki assuming her usual role as the quietly forbearing queen of the backseat. We were picking up our friend Colin, flying in from Chicago, at the Portland airport. Colin had gone to college with us and had served, over the years, as a reliable plus-one, plus-two when he had some short-lived girlfriend in tow. He was generally satisfied by what the world presented to him, which made him an excellent vacationer. He was a universal adapter.

Julia and I hadn't ceased speaking to each other, but a ten-hour drive was a long time for anyone, especially two people with particular things to not talk about. We listened to NPR through Virginia, and then I switched to music while Julia put herself to sleep with the new Saul Bellow collected essays. I was limited in my music choice to the dozen or so heavily scratched CDs in my immediate reach, *Pleased to Meet Me*, *Fear of a Black Planet*, *Sticky* fucking *Fingers*. I had the audiobook of an acclaimed surfing memoir on my phone but didn't want to hear it. I wanted, oddly enough, to *just think*, a concept foreign enough to me that it deserved the italics of a ready-made phrase from another language.

I tried to get a sexual fantasy about Leslie going—Sunday-

morning exchange of oral sex in an expensive hotel room?—
but my brain resisted full engagement. I moved on to what I
hoped might be a more productive line of thinking, mostly the
word "Maine" repeated over and over again with panicked
flashes of Leslie's face in between. Kiki sighed and shifted in the
backseat—I would need to stop and walk her around a parking
lot at least three more times before we arrived. There was such
a long way still to go.

We stopped to buy heaping sandwiches and rugelach at the
always-slammed old-fashioned deli near Hartford. Chopped liver
was the one foolproof path to Julia's heart that I knew, and I
sensed a partial, temporary détente as we ate standing over the
baking hood of the car. Kiki sat in the driver's seat, monitoring
every chunk dropped from bread to wax paper, until, yes, good
dog, she was rewarded with scraps on the asphalt.

In the car, the silence between us took on a hazier quality,
one less pregnant with the next unasked question. We listened
to a throwback hip-hop station that seemed to be permanently
playing a loop of the opening Kool & the Gang horn sample from
"Let Me Clear My Throat."

"Do you want me to read something to you?" Julia said after
about ten minutes of this.

"I think DJ Kool's going to start shouting soon," I said.

"The caveat is that I'm only going to read you something that
I'm already in the middle of, because that's what I want to read."

"What are you in the middle of?"

"Bunch of things. But the one I want to read is *The Magic
Mountain*."

"Seriously?"

"Or I could read silently to myself, like a normal person, and
you can keep waiting for the fucking *drop*."

So she read me the boring adventures of what's-his-name, a
tale I'd failed to read in a college class and again in an ill-advised

all-male book club in New York. The fact that I didn't particularly care about or for the words being spoken gave me an opportunity to savor the instrument of Julia's voice, its depth and weight, which, of course, I didn't do nearly enough. I tuned out the content completely and focused on the rise and fall of the words, the way her voice ran down at the end of a long sentence, then rose again with urgency at the start of a new one. I pictured her trudging up flights of stairs, pausing on the landings, continuing higher.

"I need to stop," she said raspily, after an hour. She gulped water from a cloudy pink Nalgene.

"That was better than I thought it'd be," I said. "Less German."

"Probably helps to have it read by an Italian Jew," she said.

Within seconds, she was asleep again—after years of medical school, I was used to this—and the spell broke. The hip-hop station had turned to static so I listened to the hits of the eighties, nineties, and today. "Today," even when expanded to include almost two decades, was not a good day. Unless that Santana song came out after the year 2000?

A few miles from the airport in Portland, I accidentally woke Julia by slamming on my brakes ahead of a traffic slowdown I hadn't noticed.

"Sorry," I said.

"You'd be even more sorry if you were picking my teeth out of the dashboard," she said. "Come *on*, man."

We inched through rush-hour traffic to the airport in that old ugly silence. Colin was waiting, with one tiny shoulder bag, at the arrivals curb.

"What's haps, *cabrones?*" he said, falling into the backseat. He tried to pet Kiki but she burrowed herself tightly against the door, poking her tongue out briefly in cottonmouthed disinterest.

"Oh, just lots and lots and lots of driving," Julia said. "Did I mention the driving?"

"What's the emotional temp?" he said. "Hopes and dreams?"

"Swimming," I said. "Lobsters. Swimming with lobsters?"

"Now, are we going to *cook* lobsters?" Colin said. "The whole gourmet-murder thing? I *do* know how, but I know, Jules, that you're not so into killing stuff."

"I *eat* lobster," Julia said. "But my parents want us to buy live ones from the neighbors, and I think I really don't want to do that?"

"I'm all right skipping it," I said.

"Well, no one thought *you* were going to be much help," Julia said. "I think it's kind of on Colin."

Silence.

"We've got to get you guys out of this car," Colin said.

"I've forgotten what it's like to *not* be in it," Julia said. "I think I might just stay."

"Don't worry, Pete and me'll make it better," Colin said. "You're the vacation princess, we're the helpers."

"I need to get a lot of writing done this week," she said. "I'm sure you helpers can find something to help with. Kiki will appreciate it."

"It's a shame Betsy couldn't come," I said to Colin. Clearly it was time to stop engaging Julia. "I wanted to meet her."

"We're pretty much broken up," Colin said. "At first it was fun to be dating this, like, Randian figure. I kind of thought she was joking a lot of the time, but it turns out she wasn't. She actually just really hates poor people. The sex is great, obviously."

"I don't think I've ever knowingly had sex with a Republican," Julia said. "It was kind of funny in college when girls were saying they'd have sex with Bush people if they promised to vote Kerry. I might've done it, but I wasn't really into having sex with random people back then."

"Yeah, once I realized how serious Betsy was about her horrible politics, I thought that maybe I'd be doing a good deed by dating her and slowly changing her mind. But I think she's rubbing off on *me*. It's like the emperor and Anakin. And you know how *that* ends."

"Peter's into assertive, morally bankrupt women these days," Julia said.

"Who isn't?" Colin said. "I'm just getting to that point where it's like, if there's literally *no chance* I'm going to settle down with this person, how long should I string it out?"

"Col, you've been saying that since you were eighteen," Julia said.

"Truer now than ever."

It was almost dark by the time we got to the house. Kiki bounded out of the car, thrilled to be free, and skidded all the way onto the dock, very nearly into the inlet. She'd still never gone swimming, always wimping out when her feet couldn't touch the bottom of a body of water. I'd vowed to finally get her all the way in on this trip, as if that were something worth prioritizing at this particular juncture.

Julia unlocked the door of the little house, which was perched right against the water, and I walked down to the dock to collect Kiki. An email from Leslie had come in while I was driving, but I'd restrained myself from checking it during the trip. Now I stole a glance.

She missed me. She was reading Don DeLillo, which wasn't helping anything. She wished she were swimming in the ocean with me, but since she wasn't, she wondered if I could give her Kenny's number so she could swim and work at his place, and also finally meet the man whose house and garden she'd enjoyed so much. She also hoped I would tie her down and fuck her for three days straight when I had a minute.

I felt a tinge about giving her Ken's number. It had to do with my sentimentalizing the five days we'd spent together out at his place, so much so that the house, in my memory, had become *mine*, not Kenny's, and the idea of her spending time with him there was therefore a *violation*. I knew this was all bullshit the moment it crossed my mind, but I still felt it. I didn't respond to Leslie's email. I called Kiki and she ducked around my heels as I brought bags and supplies in from the car. The house itself was tiny—just a kitchen, a living room, and an upstairs overtaken entirely by one large bedroom. There was a little cottage next door where Colin would be staying, a shack about the size of a boutique hotel room. It was good, I thought, that he wouldn't be a party to whatever went on between us that week.

That night, Colin and Julia cooked pasta and made sauce while I made a playlist of "good cooking songs" and drank wine.

"How's your poetry going?" Colin said to Julia.

"Oh, I don't know," Julia said. "I think it's on an upswing. Unfortunately I'm one of those people who writes better when they're unhappy. Which is a shame. I'd much rather do the 'love like a bourgeois and reveal your savage guts on the page' thing."

"I don't think that's how that goes," I said.

"Is med school bad right now?" Colin said.

"I'm just dealing with a lot of other stuff," Julia said. "*We* are."

She was standing at the stove with her back to me. I wanted to see her face. It was out of character for her to tell anyone, even Colin, about the mechanics of our relationship, and even more so to do it in a dramatic fashion. So I waited, and Colin did, too.

Finally, he said, "What do you mean?"

"Well," she said. "Oh, fuck it. Peter is . . . just tell him, would you?"

"I don't know what you're going to say," I said.

"Yes you do."

"Maybe we don't need to talk about this now," Colin said.

"Julia's upset with me because I have this intimate [Julia:

"HA!"] relationship with a friend of mine," I said. "Of ours. And she—you—feel anxious about it, which I totally understand. But we haven't talked about it that much."

"Colin, you know I'm not crazy," Julia said. "He's sleeping with this girl, or has slept with her. I'm not happy about that, obviously, but I just wish we could have a normal conversation about it."

"This is the opposite of that," I said.

"What, are you *so* worried about Colin hearing this?"

"Seriously, it's none of my business," Colin said. "I'd leave, but I really want to eat dinner. Can we just make dinner, and eat it?"

"I do understand your point," I said to Julia. "And I'm sorry for hurting your feelings."

"Hurting my feelings by doing what?"

"By being insensitive."

"Wrong," she said.

"You know what I mean," I said.

"Peter, I don't. Care. About. The sex. That much. I just want you to tell me that it happened."

"It didn't," I said.

"Well, then I'm sleeping in Colin's cabin tonight. With Colin. We're sharing the cabin. You can have this whole stupid house to yourself."

"Um," Colin said.

"Sleep wherever you want," I said. "Let's make dinner, okay?"

"Supersonic" by Oasis came up on my playlist and the ridiculousness of the song's intrusion punctured the moment. We were standing around a tiny kitchen, the three of us, having a dispute out of a Rohmer movie an hour into a week's vacation on the ocean. They finished cooking dinner, and Colin started talking about the movies he'd seen that summer, and we all feverishly talked about movies for the next hour. After we ate, we put on a recent movie about hipster vampires that Colin had brought with him. I had no particular desire to see it, but it was the closest activity to hand, and one that would involve little opportunity for further conversation. The movie ended desultorily, like it had begun, and the three of us sat there in silence, staring at the credits.

"That was okay," Colin said.

"The music was good," I said.

Silence.

"It was *awful*," Julia said cheerfully. "Am I missing something?"

"I was being diplomatic," Colin said. "Have you *seen* most movies? They're really bad."

"Duh, that's why I'm into, like, poetry?" Julia said.

She took her wineglass into the kitchen, then picked up her suitcase from where she'd left it by the front door.

"I'm going to sleep in the cabin," Julia said. "You guys stay up as late as you want." She walked out into the night.

"Boy, it's good I flew here from Chicago," Colin said.

"One of us would probably be dead by now if you hadn't," I said.

"You, I hope," he said. "What do you want me to do? I'm stuck here, you know? Like, physically."

"I want you to be here, bud. And Julia does, too. We'll start having fun, I promise."

I felt two quick buzzes in my pocket, a text message. I felt my cock getting hard just thinking about a note from Leslie.

"I don't care about having fun," he said. "I mean, I *did*, but. What's going on, man?"

I paused. I knew that I should lie, but I thought that might be the final step to my damnation, if that was a real thing. Colin deserved something like the actual truth.

"I'm seeing this girl," I said.

"Right," Colin said.

He paused, looked into his wineglass, saw that it was empty, and put it down on the floor.

"Don't fuck with Julia's head," he said. "That's the hardest thing to forgive. Break up with her if you have to. Go back to Virginia, clean out your shit. Do what you have to do."

"I'm going to talk to her," I said. "It all doesn't have to be so goddamn dramatic."

He stared at me, daring me to confess more. I looked out the window at a reflection of myself.

"Where *are* you sleeping?" he said finally. "I need to go to bed."

"You take the bed upstairs. I'll go see Julia, and if she doesn't want me there, I'll sleep on the couch."

"You can share the bed with me if you want to," Colin said. "Don't be a martyr."

He picked up his bag and bounded upstairs, taking the steps two at a time. Colin, more than anyone I knew, seemed able to change his mood instantaneously, moving from anger or sadness to complete equilibrium with no stops in between. (Julia, for better or worse, ranked second in this odd ledger.) I finally checked my phone and read Leslie's text message: "you see my email? send me kenny's # or email? miss yr face + books." Well, there was that at least. I wanted to tell her I missed her, but I sent her Kenny's number and nothing else. She didn't respond. I read a graphic novel for a while, the memoir of a middle-aged Russian woman's dating life in New York, and empathized deeply with the protagonist. I wished that I could write a quotidian memoir about my life as a woman in New York, with occasional detours to Europe and L.A. They couldn't write them fast enough for me. All the women I knew wanted to write novels with plots.

I stepped out onto the front porch and heard a faint warning bark from the guest cabin. Dogs can hear a door open from one hundred miles away. I was anticipating the worst, but when I got to the cabin, Julia was asleep or pretending to sleep. She curled toward me under the covers, instinctually or otherwise, and I warmed myself by the heat she gave off, that inefficient generator. I slept soundly, to my surprise. I dreamed about arguing.

I woke up to bright sunshine and an empty bed. It was ten a.m. I walked outside, surveyed the ridiculous beauty of the water and the coastline and the tiny island a few hundred yards away. I was mad that I couldn't enjoy it, that I'd made it impossible for myself to have a nice vacation. A vacation from *what* being the inevitable echo. It was Julia's vacation. A nice time, then. A nice fucking time, *in general*. I wanted my unhappiness to be a result of defying convention—like a Hardy novel where I'd exceeded my society's allowance for freethinking and was now being punished. But I wasn't actually that stupid. It had occurred to me lately that it was much more possible than I'd previously considered to be both "self-aware" and fundamentally wrong about the nature of the self.

I found my phone in the main house, on the couch where I'd left it. There was a Post-it note stuck to it, in Colin's handwriting. "Went for a run with J and Kiki. Coffee in the kitsch. B uv good cheer, ocean boi. C."

I turned on my phone, which was nearly dead. Nothing from Leslie. There was one form email from an obscure literary journal rejecting a half-finished story I'd sent them, and a political newsletter I received daily and never read. I sat on the front porch drinking coffee and puffing on my vaporizer until I was both seriously stoned and jittery with caffeine. I walked down to the dock and put my feet in the cold water, stretched the rest of my body out so I was taking on maximum sun. Maybe I could be happy without Leslie, if she went away. I'd been happy, or happy enough, before I met her. I still loved Julia. That wasn't really in question. I had plenty of love. It was, I was realizing, a callous kind of love. That seemed to be all I had to give. Anyone I was with would realize that eventually, I thought, with my feet in the water, so really the goal was to create the illusion of depth for as long as possible. Not for the sex, no. For the company. Other people were interesting, and the more privileged time you had with them the less bored you would be. They would teach you how to live, or at least entertain you while you failed to learn. And it wasn't entirely selfish, because, to other people, *you* were someone else, too, someone interesting, even if you knew that you weren't. I knew a lot of people who thought that everything they said and did was of value, worthy of broadcast on the local or national level. I was coming to understand that it was this belief itself that sustained those people's desire for communication, rather than the actual content of what was being said. Content, now more than ever, was irrelevant. Then Kiki was licking my face, and I felt a shadow blocking the sun over me.

"Wake up, little Susie," Colin said.

"How was your run?" I said.

"Real nice," he said. "We almost tired your dog out."

"Where's Julia?"

"Went in to get some water. We were gonna swim to that island. You down?"

"I . . . swim," I said with some hesitation.

"Know you do, son. Put on some trunks."

I sat up, turned around, and shaded my hand over my eyes to look up at Colin.

"What's Julia got to say?"

"I heard panting, mostly," Colin said. "Something about how she hopes we'll procure some seafood for tonight. Something about how she doesn't want some bullshit to ruin a week by the sea. Real WASP stuff. I guess neither of you got killed last night."

"Our lives aren't worth dying over," I said.

"You stoned? What *time* is it?"

"You guys go off for your sexy exercise, leave me here all contem*pla*tive and shit. Man's got to contemplate using the tools at his disposal."

"Let's go swimming. Unless you're going to *drown*."

"Wouldn't that be nice? Then you two can go running together to your heart's content. Once you get that fascist chick off your back."

"Seriously, go put on a bathing suit," Colin said. "And get Julia."

I hoisted myself to my feet, blinking away the dark spots in my eyes from the sunlight. Colin was a saver. He was born to save.

I didn't know where my bag was. Probably in the main house, since I didn't remember bringing it to the cabin. But maybe I hadn't taken it out of the car? Julia was probably in the cabin because that was where her stuff was, and I wanted to talk to her. But I wanted to get changed first. I didn't like the way my heart was beating, all fast and persistent, demanding an answer. But what was the question?

Julia wasn't in the main house, and neither was my bag. I did find a clementine, though. I stripped it shoddily and chewed its juices. My phone was dead. I went upstairs and plugged it into Colin's phone charger, which was plugged into the wall by the bed where I'd expected it to be. His phone was sitting there, too, and I tried to check what he'd been texting, but it was password protected. I typed in his birth date, then some random numbers, but to no avail. I went through his bag and found a swimsuit. He was significantly skinner than I was, so my belly hung over the cheap orange nylon, but I didn't care. I liked wearing Colin's stuff. It wasn't funny, exactly, just potentially aggravating in a low-key way. I picked out an Oxford University

T-shirt from his bag and put that on, too. When I got back to the dock, Julia was out there with Kiki and Colin was already in the water.

"Hey, good-lookin'," I said.

Kiki ran up and greeted me with her paws in the air, like I'd been gone for months, not minutes, then proceeded to painfully drag her claws down my back. Julia ignored me and stared out toward the water.

"Dude, it's *really* cold," she called to Colin.

"But then you go numb!" he called back.

I took off my shirt and ran past Julia into the ocean. The cold was painful, debilitating. It made me want to sink to the bottom. But I surfaced and swam over to Colin.

"Oh, my glasses!" I yelled.

"What about them?"

"I think I was wearing them when I jumped in. Oh fuck."

I dove deep near the dock, sweeping my hands through gunk and seaweed. I'd lost three pairs of glasses in bodies of water, but none since I turned fifteen. It felt inevitable, now, because I deserved everything coming to me. I came up for air in a panic.

"Peter, your glasses are right here," Julia said from the dock. "They're on top of your shirt."

"Oh," I said. "That's good."

"Calm down," she said. "Stop doing drugs."

"Get in here!" Colin yelled to Julia.

She yelled, "Fuck it!" and jumped in, then surfaced screaming. Kiki stood on the very edge of the dock howling in confusion and anxiety. Losing me to the water was one thing, but both of us gone to the depths? Unbearable.

"Okay, this is actually the worst," Julia said, though she was smiling. She looked beautiful. Thanks to endorphins, I guess, and maybe Colin, she was happy. She started swimming toward the island, kicking hard and powering onward with sharp, chopping arms. Colin glided after her, and I followed, splashing for a while in incompetent imitation of them before resorting to my usual dog paddle. Kiki's howls grew more plangent the farther we swam, and I swam on my back for a bit, watching Kiki race from one end of the dock to the other. The sound disturbed me, made my heart hurt again. I worried that she was going to fall in the water and drown trying to get back onto the dock, or trying to swim after us, and who could live with *that* on their conscience forever? The more I listened to her cries, the more I wanted to go back and placate her. Let Julia entertain whatever crypto-romantic fantasy she was conjuring about life on an eight-hundred-square-foot island with Colin. It would be something out of a contemporary magic realist story: A man sits with his dog and watches as his partner and his best friend take up a new life together on a desolate island a few hundred yards from shore. Years pass, and the narrator watches them build a house, catch fish, raise their children, all on this tiny uninhabited island, while he and the dog waste away in longing, back on the mainland. It had that perfect combination of not making any sense and being full to the brim with banal sentiment. I tried to ignore Kiki and kept swimming for the island. Dogs probably had something in their brains that kept them from killing themselves in most instances.

The island was just far enough away that I got tired and worried for all of thirty seconds that I wasn't going to be able to make it. But then, up ahead of me, I saw Julia and Colin already walking on the sandbar leading up to the island proper, and realized I could have swum twice as far. *Ten* times as far, if I had to! My knees hit rocks and shells and I bird-stepped gingerly to the sand. I looked back toward the dock and the house but without my glasses it was just an incomprehensible blur. I didn't hear barking and I didn't see movement, so I became immediately convinced that Kiki had fallen in the water and drowned and that it was my fault for overriding my valid concerns and continuing on the path of hedonistic excess instead of exercising my responsibility to the creature I'd raised from puppyhood to depend on me.

"Can anyone see?" I yelled to Colin and Julia, who had their backs to me.

"What is it?" Julia said brusquely.

"Can you see if Kiki's all right?" I said. "Is she in the water?"

"What?" Julia said. A hint of worry entered her voice. She turned around and shielded her eyes from the sun. "She's lying on the dock. Looking very sad. But she's fine."

"Where?" I said.

"Look where I'm pointing," she said, kinder. "No, there. See? That dog-shaped brown and black thing?"

"Not really," I said.

"Well, that's where she is," Julia said, walking back toward Colin. "She's fine."

I squinted hard. I hadn't been able to see that far since I was about nine years old. I had to take it on faith. Julia might not have liked me much anymore, but I knew she still loved Kiki.

I followed Colin and Julia toward the far end of the island. We passed through some scrubby grass and a couple of piney trees and then the land abruptly turned to rock, smooth at first and more jagged toward the water. We all sat on a big outcropping on the farthest, I don't know, *western* corner of the island. Some corner. Everyone was being quiet and wistful so I started talking.

"I'm thinking about how writers are, like, predestined to write whatever they're going to write?" I said. "It's stupid how people are always lamenting that Fitzgerald wasted so much of his talent on these hacky short stories or on trying to be a Hollywood screenwriter or whatever. Or people will wish that Updike had taken his time and written, like, six good novels instead of thirty okay ones. But isn't what they *did* do basically whatever they were capable of doing? I mean, being who he was, how could Fitzgerald have done anything else, right? That's the thing about alternate histories."

"First of all," Colin said. "That's *not* the thing about alternate histories. And second, all you're saying is a slightly more complicated variation on 'It is what it is,' which you say all the time."

Julia said nothing. Maybe she was looking at the blurry white thing moving swiftly across the water. A boat, probably. I wasn't the kind of person who considered boats particularly interesting or impressive, though I had a rule about always accepting invitations to board them when offered. Julia and I had watched some of the America's Cup races one summer, the year that everyone cared about it for some reason, and it was always impossible to tell what the hell was going on, even with my glasses on and the commentators explaining everything.

"I never understood why you were so into free will," I said. "It seems tacky."

"It's his secret Christian stuff," Julia said. "You were in that Milton seminar. Gotta have free will to commit original sin. *God* knows what's going to happen, but you have to be able to choose to do wrong. Or so say secret Christians."

"But what about talent?" I said.

"To be cultivated, my boy," Colin said. "Your buddy Scott really fucked the dog on that one. Most of your dead artist heroes: worse than they should have been."

"Are you being really hostile or am I more stoned than I thought I was?"

"He's hungry," Julia said. "You know how he gets."

"Let's go back," I said. "Let's save Kiki a year of therapy."

"We need to enjoy the island more," Julia said.

"It's right here," I said.

"Shhh," she said. "*Enjoy it.*"

I got up and wandered around, mostly blind. Even without eyesight, I could enjoy being warm; I could enjoy the light breeze. Mostly I could worry about Leslie, and transmute that into anxiety about the dog and Colin's bitchiness and what we would have for dinner. Leslie. In these twelve hours that I'd been cut off from her, during which I'd been enjoying, or enduring, the rank specificity of this place and the longest-tenured people in my life, she'd become an idea. She was an abstract thing I wanted, a thing that I already *had*, really, if I could keep it.

———

The day unfolded in a simulation of languor. Swimming and sun and sandwiches and beer. We were working actively to soften our edges, to radiate outward rather than burrowing deeper into individual resentments. We played Erykah Badu on a laptop on the porch. We caught up on the *LRB*.

"I'm going to my room for a bit," Julia announced in the late afternoon, pausing an extra moment to make sure that I'd taken this in. She sauntered down the steps of the porch and across the lawn in a gray wrap with skulls on it. I stared at what I was reading for a few more minutes—the fourth piece that month rotely summarizing a University Press biography of an overrated mid-century poet—then stood up myself.

"I'll put on some real pants," I said to Colin. "Then we can go to the store."

"Whatever, dude," Colin said, not looking up from his book. He was desultorily reading Margaret Atwood because she was the preferred author of the women on his online dating site.

Julia was in the shower when I went into the cabin. Kiki clawed at the door but I didn't let her in. I sat on the bed, thinking about things that would make me want to have sex with Julia. In my mental riffling, Leslie reemerged, fully formed, from the fog of abstraction in which she'd been lurking. Tangle haired, faintly sour smelling, long fingered. Real. I felt, for the first time, the sharp pang of betrayal. And I felt like I was betraying Leslie.

Julia emerged from the bathroom wrapped in a fluffy blue towel, her cheeks bright red, her shoulders and chest splotchy from the steam.

"Who gave you my room number?" she said. It was an imperious non-question. "I *specifically* told them not to admit guests."

"I'm no guest," I said, but in my normal voice. "This is *my* place."

Julia eyed me curiously. Our usual signals were scrambled, staticky.

"Then I suppose you'll be expecting the rent," she said. She put her chapped hands on her hips. It made me want to put my hands there instead, feel her sharp hip bones through the damp cotton.

"Come here," I said.

She sat down on the edge of the bed next to me, creasing herself in the middle.

"Yes?" she said.

"Where's your head at?" I said.

"My *head*? I didn't think that was what you were after."

"Where's your ass at, then? Where's your pussy been?"

I reached under the towel. She pressed my hand against her thigh.

"If you give me syphilis I'm going to fucking kill you."

———

That night, Colin and I collaborated on a seafood stew made from materials we'd purchased at an overpriced "shack" adjacent to the gigantic commercial supermarket. Julia had spent the day in one of her poetry fugues, keeping a self-enclosed vigil on the porch overlooking the ocean until I called her in for dinner, at which point she was typing in the dark, her face glowing from the light of her laptop.

"That was fast," she said absently.

"We've been cooking for like five hours," I said.

"Do we have any wine?" She stood up and stretched, rising to the tips of her toes.

"Wine, beer. Col and I have been drinking gin and tonics."

"Do I want *that?*" she said, somewhere between a rhetorical question and a genuine one.

"I'll make you one," I said. "Then you'll know."

We'd been into the gin fairly seriously since we got back from the store, and maybe it was partly the sun, but I felt floaty, medium-bodiless. It felt good. It was, I thought, a state well short of checked out. It was a mere gentling of what I would be anyway.

I'd received a long email from Leslie in the afternoon, which I read in discrete bursts over the course of the day and evening. She'd had lunch at Kenny's and they'd hit it off fabulously. He'd cooked her fish tacos and given her a slightly more coherent tour of the property. And she *loved* Scruggs, his little dog. Not as much as Kiki, of course. But Scruggs *was* a bit friendlier. She didn't feel that she was being judged quite as much by him. Anyway, they'd had some beers and made plans to hang out during the week whenever they were both free, which was most of the time. They'd talked about me, of course. She hadn't told Kenny explicitly what was going on between us, but he inferred it, and it seemed like he approved. He told her that he was "morality neutral" when it came to sex, so long as "nobody acted like an asshole," which seemed to be a contradiction. Then she talked about *Underworld* for a while, which I hadn't read, so didn't find particularly interesting, and then she signed off.

I knew, or thought I knew, that she wouldn't have sex with

Kenny, but their reported intimacy made me unhappy anyway. My conception of her was that of someone who did not enter into relationships lightly, this despite the fact that our own partnership could not have been more blithely ratified. There was a school of thought that suggested it might be clarifying if Leslie turned out to be just as into Ken as she was into me; it would be a simple lesson learned about the wiles of freethinking women. They weren't to be trusted! But you could still trust the feelings of someone who slept around. *I* still deserved trust, some kind of trust, right? I was almost enlightened enough to see Leslie as I saw myself, as a soul not entirely governed by the actions of the body she happened to inhabit.

Our fish stew turned out to be pretty good, though I couldn't have re-created it if given a million opportunities. We toasted Maine; we toasted ourselves. I felt that we, as a table, had figured something out, some way of being that might somehow be sustainable if we kept our minds open, our brains flexible. We played the first-sentence game, making up possible opening lines to the middlebrow novels of later-life coastal love that Julia's parents kept in the house. By the third round, our entries had descended fully into the realm of the bizarre: Julia's tended to contain mathematical symbols, mine were in pidgin Italian. You had to be there.

Later, we lay on the dock, looking at the sky. There seemed to be far more shooting stars than usual that night, but maybe it had just been a long time since we'd been somewhere we could see the sky clearly. Spotting stars became competitive. I was pretty sure Colin was pretending half the time, but I knew Julia was being honest, and she was still seeing a lot more than I was. By two a.m., even those two dedicated joggers were bumming smokes from my emergency pack. I'd miss both of them, I thought.

Julia and I went back to the cabin at the end of the night.

"We can work this out, right?" she said. "You wouldn't choose some girl you just met over me. You're not that kind of person."

"I know," I said. "I'm going to fix it."

I'd decided to end things with Julia in a week, when we got back to Charlottesville.

Part VI

J ulia and I broke up for the first time a year after we graduated from college. We were living in New York, separately, me in a fifth-floor walk-up in Clinton Hill, her in a two-bedroom occupied by four people on 128th Street in Manhattan. The commute was so ridiculous that we tried to coordinate which apartment we would stay at for two or three days at a time, but inevitably something vital was left in one place or the other, requiring round-trip A train rides so long that one could read an entire late-period Roth novel.

We had been arguing, since a month into our dating life, about the fact that Julia had slept with only one other person besides me, and even that had been only a one-night stand with a hirsute Bulgarian floor-mate her freshman year. Think of all she'd be missing if we stayed together forever! The speculation hadn't bothered me that much at first. We were mostly happy together, and it seemed premature to the point of irrelevance to be worrying about a sexual lifetime. But it kept coming up.

One night, after a movie at which we'd consumed a large Poland Spring bottle's worth of vodka, Julia was particularly persistent in speculating about the skill and stamina of our friend Connor, who was, it must be noted, very handsome and an apparently excellent rock climber. At some point, she edged from speculation to intention.

"I bet he'll be really creative," she said. "And, like, strong, but gentle. Not *demanding*, you know, but, like, with a clear knowledge of his own body."

"I know my body," I said. "Shin bone, hip bone. Hippocampamus."

"Different doesn't mean *better*," she said. "It's fun to think about it. Isn't that what you're doing when you jerk off?"

"I'm always thinking of you," I said. "I'm thinking of your face."

"You're not as funny as you think you are," she said. She was sitting on the edge of the bed. I was lying on the floor.

"If you need to get fucked by whoever, who am I to stop you?" I said. "Just like take a shower at his place before you come over, you know?"

"I have my own place," she said, calm. "And you're in it, unfortunately."

I stood up suddenly and the blood rushed from my head. I steadied myself against her dresser, knocking over a pile of books. I was so drunk that I thought I was sober. I eyed the books that had formed a collapsed ziggurat. *The Waves* by Virginia Woolf was nearest to hand. It was Julia's favorite book at the time. I'd borrowed her copy of it for months and made it through ten heavily underlined pages before giving up in baffled boredom. Now I picked it up.

"You think Virginia Woolf worried about how many people she'd fucked?" I said.

"Yes," Julia said.

I tore the book in half—it came apart at the spine much faster than I thought it would—and dropped the pieces on the floor.

"Oh, shit," Julia said quietly.

I walked out of the bedroom and out the front door. I walked for a long time, all the way to the Forty-Second Street subway, with a dull thud in my ears—*You're fucked, you're fucked, you're fucked*. Times Square was at its empty, bathetic worst, wasted electricity for the sad-about-sex.

When I finally got to Brooklyn I'd sobered up enough to realize the scale of my failure. I had a long email from Julia waiting in my inbox. It was comprehensive, accurate, damning. It's a bad sign when a person who has every reason to be furious with you opens a letter with two paragraphs about your good qualities ("You like good country music. You are caring and adept with animals. You are neither overly nor too little concerned with the getting and spending of money"). It is the mark of someone who has taken your full measure and found it wanting.

In the third paragraph, Julia laid it out: despite my kind and noble qualities, my ego prevented me from making a sincere connection with her, and thus from understanding and fulfilling her needs. She recommended that I use the next period of my life, "of whatever duration," to examine my heart and attempt to understand what I wanted from myself and from a partner, and that I "not merely grab on to the nearest person like a drowning shipwrecked sailor clings to passing driftwood."

She concluded with the exhortation that I "be better." Not for her, mind you, and not for my next partner, but—get this—for myself. But wasn't I *already* too self-involved? Wasn't that the foremost of my myriad problems?

We were broken up for a year and a half, during which time Julia joined and quit Teach for America, and finally got to find out that sex with young men was all pretty much the same. I got my first magazine job and tried desperately to date a fellow assistant who knew better, then dated one of her friends in defeat. Julia and I got back together after crashing into each other at a Titus Andronicus concert at Maxwell's. It was, in retrospect, too easy.

Upon our return from Maine, Julia started a two-week "independent study" block. She was supposed to be scouring hospital records for a research project on antibiotic-resistant infections, but mostly she went on long runs with Kiki at the hottest points of the day, otherwise closing herself in the shared office (which neither of us ever used, usually) and blasting *Illmatic* on repeat. She emerged only after dark to watch movies projected on our living room wall. I was too guilty to do anything but observe this from the dining room table, where I stared at Word documents and tried to find the language to mercifully sever us from each other.

Leslie and Kenny were waiting for me out at his house. I hadn't told them exactly when I would do the breaking up, but Leslie had practically moved in with Kenny, so it wasn't much of a hassle for her to be on call there. Leslie was frank about the fact that she and Ken had shared a bed on a few nights when they'd both gotten too drunk to see straight, but they both swore that nothing more significant had happened. I didn't quite believe them, but who was I to envy them their supposedly straightforward affection, stuck as I was in my pantomime of commitment?

"Come watch?" Julia called to me on the fourth night of this.

"What's on?" I said. I stood in the doorway of the dining room, not meeting her eyes. She was wearing a football-themed fake-vintage Rolling Stones T-shirt.

"I don't know," she said. "Is there anything you want to see?"

"Um," I said. I tried to think of something normal. All we ever watched were foreign films about the inevitable dissolution of relationships. "We still haven't watched that movie about the Indonesian genocide."

She searched my face to see if I was joking. I wasn't sure myself.

"Didn't you want to see that Renoir movie about India?" she said. "That probably wouldn't be horrible."

I had wanted to watch that, at some point. I'd wanted to do a lot of things.

"Sure," I said. "Do you want a beer?"

"Naw," she said, tapping at her keyboard blankly, finding us the fun. From the kitchen I heard music, presumably the opening of the movie, a rhythmic sitar-like humming. A plummy British accent was saying something pedantic about India. The *tone* of the fucking thing . . .

I came back empty-handed and landed heavily in the armchair across from Julia.

"Hey, look," I said.

She kept her eyes on the wall, on the movie. The voice-over prattled on until she suddenly lunged and struck the space bar on her computer, stopping the sound. She finally turned to me, her face glowing deep blue from the light of the power button on the projector.

"I'm keeping Kiki," she said.

I had considered this. When we first adopted her, Julia and I had made a verbal canine prenup in the event of just such a thing occurring. Because I had been the one most stricken with the need for a dog, it had been decided that I would become her guardian in the event of a breakup or a period of long separation due to career, family illness, etc. We'd joked about the arrangement with friends—it seemed, to us, if not to them, a sign of our progressiveness, or something, to be able to talk openly about what would in reality be an extremely unhappy situation. I had resolved to myself that I would be gracious in this matter. I told myself that I'd done the hard math and concluded that Leslie and the open future were more important than a dog who was so braided into my daily life that I sometimes went a week without really thinking about her. But now that Julia had said it out loud, I felt nauseous with despair. Is there anything more pathetic than imagining your dog waiting by the door for you to come home, wagging her tail brightly at the sound of a similar car coming down the street, only to hang her head in shame when you don't arrive? Or, the obvious facing image in the pendant, the dog growing accustomed to your absence, then, eventually, shifting her loyalty? There was some small comfort to be found in Kiki's steadfast resistance to strange men. Perhaps she would drive more than one suitor away with her attitude. Which was a terrible thing to want, too.

"You should have her," I said. "I know."

I started crying and put my head in my hands. When I looked up, Julia was still perched on the edge of the couch, holding the resolute expression that I knew did not come naturally to her. Kiki was under the bed, probably. She could sense bad vibes coming from a long way off.

"I'm really sorry," I said to Julia, wiping my tears with the palms of my hands. There really weren't that many tears.

"You need to go," she said. "I know you're going to regret this, and it's going to be a real fucking shame. I don't even hate you yet, so I mostly just feel sad for you. What you're doing is awful, and I'm not going to forget it."

"I wouldn't do it if I didn't have to," I said.

"That's got resonance, Pete," Julia said. "You should be a writer. You should fucking write something down on a piece of paper."

And, what? I would have liked to say something worthy of the life we'd shared, but that's not what happened. I got up and walked quickly to the bedroom, threw some dirty clothes in a bag. I grabbed a couple of books I wasn't reading from the bedside table. What better time to finally crack *A Dance to the Music of Time*? I tried to coax Kiki out from under the bed but she wouldn't budge. She was scared; she didn't recognize me like this. Or maybe she just thought I wanted to give her a bath.

W hen I got out to Kenny's house, he and Leslie were already standing on the front lawn. They took turns hugging me in silence. I'd texted to alert them of my imminent arrival, but there was still something unsettling to me in their solemn reception, somewhere between the taking in of a fugitive and acknowledging a mourner at a wake. Then Scruggs raced out the front door and I started crying again.

"Aw, buddy," Kenny said. "Let's get some whiskey in you. We're not gonna talk about the bad times no more."

"I'll go in and turn off the George Jones," Leslie said.

"Seriously?" I said.

"Naw, we were listening to the Everly Brothers," Kenny said. "Bet you can guess the tune."

I took a seat on the flowered, yellowing couch next to Leslie. Ken poured me a coffee mug of bourbon.

"Well, what've you guys been doing?" I said. I took a sip of the whiskey. I didn't want to, but I started feeling like less of an asshole almost immediately.

"The same thing we do every day, Pinky," Leslie said. She

shaded southern in imitation of Kenny. "Readin', ponderin'. The intellectual country life."

"Who you calling a in-tuh-lectual?" Kenny said. "I'm just glad you're here now, Pete, so I've got somebody to make *love* to me."

"Seriously, though," Leslie said, nuzzling my shoulder with her chin. "I got a lot done. But I bet you can make me more productive."

"*That's* romantic," I said.

"Oh, right," she said. "Let's talk about romance."

After a couple of rounds, Leslie and I wandered off to the dusty downstairs bedroom that she'd taken over as her own. It was like the room of a neglected child in a particularly downcast British film: Kenny's broken instruments and power tools and a couple of Scruggs's ripped-up toys looked to have been left wherever they'd fallen on the scuffed wood floor. Leslie had countered by strewing her clothes and books around in a similarly unpremeditated fashion, and the room now had a wistful trace of her distinctive smell, an admixture of cooked vegetables, laundry detergent, and body-crevice musk.

"So are you, like, *out* out of your aunt's place?" I said.

"I've still got some stuff there," she said. "I told her I'm working on an art project that meets at night a lot, so I'm staying with a girlfriend? In the old sense of the word. I was very vague, but she seems pretty good with me being gone. She texts like every three days. Sorry, I know you must feel bad."

"I think I'm not feeling it for real yet," I said. "I mostly feel bad about losing the dog."

"Eh, bitch never liked me anyway," Leslie said. "Sorry, that's awful. Even if that's her scientific name, she's a wonderful creature. Maybe you can do joint doggie custody?"

"Don't worry about it," I said.

We sat in silence for a minute. That would have been the

time to leave. *I'm sorry, I can't do this.* And go where? Into the woods. Yes. Live in a tree. Die on the ground.

"Well, do you wanna fool around a little?" she said. "Would that make you feel better?"

I hung my head. Forest death faded as an option. But I didn't want to seem *easy.*

"Probably not," I said.

"Ohhh-kay," Leslie said.

"You didn't really want to have sex with Kenny, right?" I said.

"What do *you* want the answer to be?" She put her hand on my knee.

"For you to only want me forever?" I said.

"Now, that wouldn't be very much fun, would it? Just wanting one thing? Maybe I'm filled right up to the brim with him right now."

"You're not."

"I said maybe. The point is, you don't get to find out. You get to ask, and then I don't tell you."

"That's a little one-sided."

"Exactly. There is only my side. And lucky for you, you get to be on it."

"I'm pretty sure you have at least two sides. In my experience."

"Hey, there will be plenty of time for all that. We're having a philosophical discussion now. How many sides are there?"

"One?"

"Good. Good learning."

That night I lay awake until dawn, watching the morning light bring texture and shade to the contours of Leslie's snoring nose.

W e started life as a family of three. During the day, Leslie and I found corners in which to do or not do our work while Kenny went into town to work day shifts at the soup place or rehearse with his band. Then we all joined up for dinner, cooked, more often than not, by Kenny. Leslie was somehow even less inclined toward the kitchen arts than I was, bored to death by the idea of a recipe and cheerfully incompetent at improvisation. Together, we managed pasta with red sauce and, another time, a gloppy stir-fry almost inedibly heavy on peanut butter.

"I mean, it's *food*," Kenny said, setting on the latter dish.

Leslie worked hard in the stifling house, commandeering the rickety wooden table by the big window in the front room. She'd angled an old metal floor fan to blow directly into her face, sending her hair into a constant storm around her head and, not co-incidentally, rendering her deaf to the world. She could put in four, maybe five hours before breaking for a swim, which I was always more than ready to join her in.

I decided my best shot at productivity was to isolate myself upstairs, in the room whose closet had previously housed the three-legged kitten. (Kenny had given him to the cute girl who

worked at the bookstore when he tired of its pissing on the bed.)
This was the hottest room in the house, but I was going for some
kind of masochistic hypnotism, imagining that my intense physical
discomfort might somehow lead to an aesthetic breakthrough.
There was no Wi-Fi up there, nothing on the walls, no books. The
morning started bearable, a decent breeze wafting through the
one small window. I opened a story I'd been working on for
years, a thing about a secretly gay Republican congressman, and,
reading through it, became increasingly distressed by the rever-
berating yammer that sounded nothing like the voice in my
head. What was the point of writing if all you ended up with was
this, the textual equivalent of a speakerphone voicemail overheard
on a bus?

I put the story aside and added it to the growing list of things
I was inadequate at or incapable of doing. I couldn't tie a knot
more complicated than a shoelace. I couldn't roll a good joint,
drive stick, or shuffle cards. I couldn't string or tune, let alone
play, any instrument. I couldn't juggle anything, dice a vegetable, shotgun a beer, or ride a bicycle in even moderate traffic. I
couldn't do a somersault, sing or whistle a tune, follow a map,
or dance any recognized dances. I could not take a photograph
of distinction, couldn't draw or paint an identifiable subject. Almost anything considered a sport was basically a wash. I was uncomfortable handling guns and fireworks—anything on fire or
remotely combustible, really. I had no idea how the stock mar-
ket worked. I was afraid to try the really interesting drugs. There
was a long history of mental illness in my family.

At this point I realized that I was on the verge of passing out
from the heat, so I went downstairs to gulp water from a jar in
the kitchen and stare at Leslie, with her discipline and flying
hair. I did my best not to bother her, but I'm sure my hunched,
imploring presence, even if unacknowledged, was not helpful. I
returned to my hundred-degree prison to squint through sweat

into my dirty screen until Leslie called me down for a trip to the pond, where we floated around making desultory conversation about books and the people who wrote them. The sphere of reference shrank slowly, from Dickens and Tolstoy to Díaz and Cusk, to people we knew and then, inevitably, with relief, ourselves.

"I think I could, like, *do* this," Leslie said, floating on her back while I treaded water. "It's not, you know, *there yet*, but I'm peeking around a corner. There's a ton of stuff the next room over. Worlds, maybe."

"Sure, that's how it feels when it's going *well*," I said.

"But even when it's not, there's this buzzing lately. There's some usable static coming through."

"It's all the future applause," I said.

"The crickets, maybe," Leslie said. "There are like twenty good readers left in America; I'm not nuts. But maybe they'd actually read my shit if I keep fucking with it."

"It'll be cool when you're famous," I said. "I'm looking forward to being a kept man. More of one, I mean."

Leslie let her head sink under the water, stayed under for a solid ten seconds, and then rose slowly, water pouring off of her like a creature from the deep.

"I was trying to think of the funniest writer couple for us to be, where one is really good and the other just whines all the time, but I couldn't get to it quickly enough."

"Huh," I said. "That wasn't nice."

"You should send me what you've got," she said. "We'll talk it out."

"Imagine me going underwater but never coming back up," I said.

"It's your early work, man. It's allowed to be terrible. I promise I'll still like you even if it's garbage. Maybe I'll like you even more! Some chicks dig bad writers. That's a statistical fact."

This did not make me more eager to show her my writing.

We hauled ourselves onto the dock and tossed the tennis ball into the pond for Scruggs, who persisted in kamikaze dives and slow, furious dog paddles with the ball jammed between his tiny jaws, hacking up pond water, until we refused to throw it again for fear of his drowning in exhaustion. Leslie had her notebook out there and scrawled and dripped into it at irregular intervals. I stared at the sky, hoping talent was, contrary to available medical evidence, sexually transmittable.

Back in the house we ate leftover soup from Kenny's restaurant. I usually took mine cold, given the conditions inside, but Leslie heated hers on the stove.

"In Turkey, they drink hot tea even when it's hot, right?" she said. "It's good for you. It maintains equilibrium."

I thought it probably had more to do with a historical lack of ice. Out of respect for her people, I didn't bring up the genocide.

In the afternoons, I wrote emails to my family and to my friends in New York from the one corner of the house that had Internet service—cooler, just, than my upstairs hell-box—narrating my eventful summer. The shortest and least detailed email I sent received the longest response, and it was the only one that objected strongly to my choices. It was from my father, from whom, in my adult life, I had probably received no more than a couple hundred total words of text across all possible formats (emails, birthday cards, text messages). He wrote that he was worried for me, that I had "shown a potential for a very good future" with Julia, but now he did not know "what my life journey would consist of." There was something both touching and upsetting in the apparent intensity of his feelings and the bluntness with which he expressed them. "You know I love you very much and will do anything to help you. You are a good man and I am proud of you but a good man also needs a wife who will be strong and is a good person both as a wife and in her own passions and skills. I know you must have serious differences for you to end the relationship and I trust you to make good choices. Julia is a very good and smart person and maybe you will be able to reconcile with her after some time apart. I'm sure this new person is interesting to you, and what is important is that you are happy."

It went on like this for quite a while, repeating the same ideas in similar, stark language without much variation. I didn't trust my father's judgment on this matter, really, but it was sobering, nonetheless, to be its recipient. He'd always been unusually attached to Julia, and it seemed clear to me now that he'd been using my relationship with her as a proxy for my well-being and potential for future happiness. Julia, for all of her minor flaws, was a successful person. I was not going to be a doctor or a lawyer; nor, apparently, was I going to marry one. I was, basically, a squalling baby, though I didn't even squall that much. I was a needy yet eerily quiet baby.

And, anyway, Julia had not gotten in touch.

On the Friday night of my second week in the country, Molly Chang came over with her heavily bearded new boyfriend, or whatever he was. He introduced himself, in a thick Virginia accent, as Robert, but Molly called him Blob. Kenny and I—Kenny, mostly—had built a bonfire, and we all stood around it smoking a pack of Parliaments that Blob, bless his heart, was generous enough to share with us.

"But you guys aren't, like, *committed* to anything long-term, right?" Molly said to Leslie and me. "Why restrain yourselves? You just got out of these mega relationships. Have some fun."

"Well, we kind of got out of them for each other," I said.

"The provisional life is easily unmade," Molly said. "That sounds like it's been translated. But I don't know. In the poly community—which I am *not* a part of even though many of the people I've fucked recently *are*—they're very into setting boundaries. You can't have freedom without rules, because it's human nature to try to dominate the lives of others. So you make all of these stipulations in order to avoid falling under the tyranny of despotic individuals. Like America, before neoliberalism."

"Some people like falling under tyranny," I said.

"*Most* people, by the numbers," said Molly. She threw her cigarette into the fire. "I guess I've spent a lot of time trying to find
ways to be exceptional."

"And let me tell you, Molly girl, you've succeeded," Kenny
said. He put his arm around her and she leaned back against him
comfortably. Kenny'd just met her, but he'd been going out of
his way to flatter her at every opportunity since she'd arrived.
Blob seemed to lack the will, or maybe just the inclination, to
intervene.

"What do you do, Robert?" Leslie said.

"Kindergarten teacher," he said. "Love those little fuckers."

"That must be hard," I said. "I have enough trouble keeping
college students in line."

"Eh, their brains are still just malleable enough that you can
distract 'em with songs and games and shit," he said. "They don't
even know they're learning most of the time."

"I guess that's good," Leslie said.

Blob shrugged and lit a new cigarette.

"Kids think they hate school," he said with resignation. "It's
the cartoons, I guess."

"I always loved school," I said. "I wanted it to last all night."

"Hey, I'm gonna stay forever if they'll let me," said Blob. "You
guys like drugs?"

He passed around a baggie of dried mushrooms and we each
took a respectable taste, "just enough to make the fire burn a
little brighter," in Kenny's formulation. Molly declined; *someone*
had to drive the car home, she said, though I thought the chances
of their leaving the property that night were low and getting
lower.

"You *want* to go to Missoula, right?" Leslie said to me some
time later. "If I get the job?"

We were sitting off to ourselves in lawn chairs, staring at

the fire. I had that sense, often triggered by hallucinogens, of the importance of being exactly where I was, the quiet certainty that this one particular patch of ground was crucial to my well-being.

"Missoula is very, very far away," I said. "I literally cannot imagine it right now."

"Right, I know," Leslie said. "But remove the, um, physical question. The question of what the physical experience will consist of. Do you want, in, um, not theory I guess, but, like, principle—principle to be acted on, though—do you want to *do* what I do? Which is go to Missoula?"

Trying to contemplate all of that set me trembling with anxiety, but the unaffected, lizard part of my brain understood quite firmly that it was important I get my answer right.

"I don't care about my life," I said. I paused, meaning to say more, then decided to stick with that.

"Huh," she said. "Okay."

We stared at the fire for a while. Molly wandered over and flopped down at our feet. She leaned her head back into Leslie's lap, and Leslie started absently petting her long hair.

"Everyone's too nice to me," Molly said. "I think I need to be stood up to more."

"Kenny's good at standing," I said. "Seen him stand for hours."

"He is an actual puppy," Molly said. "Like, I could put him in my backpack and he'd be fine with that."

"Where is he?" Leslie said. "Are he and Robert getting along?"

"Yeah, they're bonding over, like, who has the more desiccated liver and who gets my mouth," Molly said. "Hint: not Blob."

"What about *meeeeeee?*" Leslie said.

"You crazy kids," Molly said. "You don't even know what dedication *is*."

I tried using my powers from the mushrooms to make Molly and Leslie merge into a single ectoplasmic being, a spider of limbs

and hair. It was surprisingly difficult. They remained two separate, overlapping humans. But at least I would not have to meet
my God without having tried.

"I do find it frustrating how prone men are to hysteria,"
Leslie was saying to Molly. "My father, he's got it bad. Start him
on, I don't know, 'family' or 'America' and you're looking at a
broken man."

"Definitely," Molly said. "My father's dead."

I wandered over to Ken and Blob. Kenny was drinking directly from a bottle of Old Grand-Dad, gratuitously swishing the
whiskey around in his mouth and gargling before swallowing it.
He handed the bottle to me and I took a small sip, just enough
to burn my lips.

"You doing okay?" he said.

"I think so," I said. "Hard to tell these days."

"You've got that old northern defect," he said. "Can't drink
away the foreknowledge of death."

"I guess I didn't realize it was regional," I said.

"All grievances are local," said Blob. He stared searchingly
into the fire. "Couple years ago, I would've jumped over this
motherfucker. That's not me right now. I've lost a lot of shoulder
mobility. Starts to catch up with you. Now it's like, no matter
how much you may want to ride somebody's motorcycle when
you're drunk or whatever, just, like, fucking, *don't*."

"That makes a lot of sense," I said.

"Pete here's gonna move off to Montana, leave us all behind,"
Kenny said. "Forget about all of his old hometown buddies on
the football team slash assembly line."

"No shit?" Blob said.

"We're talking about it," I said.

"Long way," Kenny said. "Long, long way."

"I'll be back, man," I said. "It's not like I'm going to prison,
you know?"

"Might as well be," Kenny said. "Leaving me all alone here, nobody to talk to. Liable to take to *drink*."

"The whole point is love," I said, unhinged with whatever was moving around in my body. "All of these things are as nothing if you do not have love. You know my great-uncle was a priest? When he died there was a priest *parade*. Drank himself to death. Maybe that was unclear. *I* liked him, anyway."

"I do admire your definitude," said Blob. "With regard to your feelings, I mean. I was quite nearly married. Man, were we nonfunctional. We did not. Function. It was like, oh, we've found the still, dead center of things. This is the quiet middle place where nothing can be done. I've never had that experience otherwise. She was a very dark person. It really infected my worldview. It's something that you shouldn't have to live with, if it isn't yours. Your own darkness. It needed to become a choice. I haven't loved a lot of people. But I wanted to live. I'm a lifer, I guess."

"What about Molly?" I said. I glanced over toward the women.

"I would say that she, too, has chosen life," Blob said. "I think we're just two random atoms, though. Not, like, chemically bonded. Is that what atoms do? God, I used to *teach* chemistry. Oh well. *You* and Molly seem awfully, um, complementary," he said to Kenny.

"Aw, I'm just being friendly," Kenny said. "I try not to get between things."

"For all of my flaws, I am not a jealous man," Blob said. "The affections of women are instruments of infinite complexity. I will not presume to measure them by the dogged dreams of man."

"Bob, I don't know who dropped you off," Kenny said. "But you're all right with me." He handed him the whiskey bottle and I realized that what had momentarily seemed to me a generous gesture on Kenny's part was in fact intended primarily to incapacitate his rival. In Kenny's eyes, Blob had demonstrated his inadequacy to be Molly's lover by failing to competently challenge Kenny's encroachments. Having established this, he was now free to seduce Molly, the most humane path to which involved putting the other guy out of his misery. The mechanics of getting and keeping, of being loved or rejected for reasons within or beyond one's control, were prominent in my mind. I was thinking a lot about whether there were universal principles at play in such things. It was hard to say. Most of the people I associated with considered themselves exceptional.

Leslie and Molly wandered over and joined us. I stood behind Leslie, hugged her back tightly to my chest, breathed deeply of her greasy hair. I tried hard to believe I knew and understood her, that I hadn't, mostly, projected my desires onto her and, as a result, had them projected right back at me. I did not have a definite sense of what time it was or where we were physically in space. I looked to my left and saw Kenny making out quite fervently with Molly. Bob was sitting cross-legged a small distance from them, staring into the fire. Oh, and Leslie was making out with me! And, what felt like hours later, we were sitting with Bob, who was passed out, watching Kenny, fully nude, languidly fuck Molly on the ground. At some point Leslie was scraping her palm over my zipper. It shouldn't have felt good, and it didn't really, but I was pleased by the activity anyway. She was not, I found shortly, wearing any underwear beneath her sundress. Was it the one she'd been wearing the night I met her? Had that dress been yellow with little blue flowers on it? Was it all right to make it so, retroactively, to make this moment more freighted with significance?

"I love that dress," I said.

"I found it in the house," she said. "It's way too small for me. You can see I'm like busting out of it."

I became convinced, with no actual memory or knowledge to back it up, that it was Julia's dress that she'd left at the house some night. It was far from impossible, since we'd stayed over together a dozen times, though it was so on the nose that it was much more likely to be a product of my misfiring brain than reality. Nevertheless, it retained an allure, the notion that Leslie's parts had been rubbing up against whatever of Julia's corporeal presence remained in the fabric. There was also a maybe dubious excitement bound up in the revelation of constraint, of Leslie, this gloriously proportioned woman, trapped in the garment of a more politely circumscribed one, like Alice after she drinks from the bottle that makes her big.

"Is it uncomfortable?" I said.

"Little bit," she said. "Thought it was cute, though. You didn't notice until just now."

"It required a certain moment," I said. "Just one particular second when I could appreciate and articulate how good you looked in some other girl's dress."

Leslie's eyes shaded skeptical; she was trying to measure how serious, or how far gone, I was. I was both, both. I felt a surging desire for the world that might have been directly connected to the knowledge that we would all smell like woodsmoke for the rest of the weekend.

The next morning, we found Molly and Kenny eating black beans and scrambled eggs at the kitchen table. Molly was wearing purple boy shorts and a T-shirt that said "Kieslowski" in glitter; Kenny was shirtless in blue jeans.

"Hey there, kids!" he called. "Breakfast on the stove. Don't eat too much. We're trying to put some meat on old Molly-bones here."

"That is *not* what we are doing," Molly said. "I don't even eat breakfast."

"You do in this house, missy," Kenny said. "Take a bite."

"Why don't you make me?" she said.

"You want me to feed you like a baby?"

They stared each other down until Molly started laughing, a deep, raspy "huh huh huh" I'd never heard from her before. She scooped some eggs into her mouth and beamed at us.

"Yo L," she said. "I hit."

I looked out the front window and saw that Bob's car was still parked in the driveway. I wondered if he would remain as magnanimous in the morning as he had been last night.

"Do you love me like Molly loves Kenny?" I said in the kitchen.

"Big gap teeth and all," Leslie said. "Do you wish I had a big gap like Molly does?"

Bob wandered in through the front door while we were finishing breakfast. He had, it transpired, slept in his car.

"How you feeling?" Leslie said. "You need some aspirin?"

"Took too much," Bob said, shaking his head in a failed approximation of wry bemusement. "I . . . I took a lot of things. The car was very heavy in the crabs department. I knew somewhat it wasn't real. I'm not a spring chicken in that regard. Even the patently nonexistent can be quite alarming. That's something we talk about at school. God, it's definitely not a school day, right?"

"I think it's Saturday," Molly said.

There was a pause as we all checked this hypothesis against our tattered mental calendars.

"That's right," I said finally. "I got the email from the *Times Book Review* yesterday, and it always comes on Friday. So it must be Saturday."

This was silently accepted as a reasonable way to measure the passage of time.

"There should be some beans and eggs left," Kenny said. "Lemme make you a plate, brother."

"Don't be friendsy with me, dude," Bob said. "All's fair, you know, no one's denying that. But let's just skip friendsy time."

Kenny held his gaze, something I don't believe I'd have been able to do.

"The food's on the stove if you want it," he said. "Nothing else needs to happen here."

"I'm not trying to be an asshat," Bob said. "But I'm not like *canonized* yet, you know? Hey, you know, Molly?"

"Okay, Robert," Molly said. "We're barely even dating. Please don't become overstimulated at me."

"Right," Bob said. "That's fine, actually. I am not handling myself well. I will just see y'all around. Somebody'll take Molly somewhere, right?"

"Yeah, for sure," Leslie and I said, just out of sync.

"Okay, thanks," he said. "Cool. Um. I'm fine to drive, right? What time is it? Eleven? That should be fine, right?"

Molly had turned away from him, concentrating on a whirling robin out the window.

"Well, everybody be well," Bob said. "Enjoy the rest of your weekend."

He kept standing there for a while.

On Monday, Leslie got a call from the head of the Montana English department. As she soon told me, despite the fact that he'd promised her the job when they spoke two weeks earlier, he was calling to say that they had, in fact, decided to go with another candidate, a guy who already lived in Montana, and had written many books about living in Montana. I was in the study at the end of the hall when she took this call, but I went to our bedroom when I heard the crash that turned out to be her phone knocking over Ken's broken guitar.

"Mother*fuckers*," she said.

"I know," I said. "It's their loss."

I felt a gigantic relief. I'd had no idea how badly I had not wanted to go. I didn't say: this gig essentially fell into your lap in the first place. She stared me down like I'd said it anyway, and I didn't doubt that she could read my mind.

"You know I love it there," she said. "I'm sure I never fucking shut up about it. It's where I wanted to finish writing this *shit*. I know it's stupid. I'm fully aware of being stupid."

She sat down on the edge of the bed, her eyes pointed past me, at the far corner of the room.

"This just means that we have more choices to make," she

said quietly. "Which is cool. It's good to choose things, instead of just doing them."

"We could pay Kenny some more rent and stay here for a while, probably," I said.

"It's too much," Leslie said. "I feel like we're under siege here or something. And, honestly, I don't think it would be nice to Kenny. I know he wouldn't admit it, especially not to you, but he's definitely still a little too into me. Things got, like, pretty close to happening when you were in Maine. He's a good guy, and I wasn't doing much to discourage it. But I knew it would be a shit show if you actually broke up with Julia and I was like, uh, by the way, me and Ken . . . But anyway, I think that's a big part of the Molly thing, too. Like, showing he doesn't need me."

"I think," I said carefully, "that he'll speak up if he's got some kind of problem."

"*I've* got a problem," she said. "That's what I'm telling you. Can we get stoned now? Please don't tell Kenny I told you that."

"I don't think it'll come up," I said. "And I don't have any weed. You want a beer? I could have a beer."

"I'm upset."

"I'm trying to make you feel better," I said. "You want me to put on 'Emotional Rescue'?"

She grabbed a book off of the floor—one of the Coetzee autobiographies that we were both reading out of sequence, in a different order—and brushed past me out of the room. I heard the front door slam, leaving me alone in the room with the rest of our paltry shit.

By dinner, we'd both calmed down, or at least mutually committed to pretending to do so. Kenny made catfish and grits, and the meal was taken up with a lighthearted discussion of all the places we could move to (North Carolina, New Mexico, the South of France). Things inevitably seemed more manageable with food and alcohol in us. Notably, Ken did not suggest we stay with him indefinitely.

"Let's go somewhere *now*," Leslie said. "We're not just doll-house people, you know?"

I was dipping a stale chocolate chip cookie into a mug of reheated coffee. I don't think I would have minded being a doll-house person, whatever that was.

"Where do you want to go?" I said.

"Let's go to Richmond. Let's go *dancing*."

"It *is* Monday," Kenny said. "Not that I'd ever tell y'all not to go nuts."

It was an hour and change to Richmond, and I didn't want to have to drive back.

"It's a *city*," Leslie said. "Worst case, we'll hang out at a bar for a couple of hours. With, like, other humans. Remember other humans?"

"Hey, I resemble that implication," Ken said.

"Maybe we'll find, I don't know, a sex party," Leslie said. "Eyes wide shut, baby?"

"I don't think that's a Richmond thing," I said. "Maybe in the Confederate graveyard, I guess."

"I'd fuck a ghost soldier right about now," Leslie said. "Union only, though."

The girl wanted to go to Richmond. I drank my coffee down to the gritty bottom of the cup and followed her out to the car.

When we made the turn onto Cary Street, the one part of the city that I knew at all well, it was quiet, if not quite ghostly, Confederate or otherwise. We parked and walked the sidewalk, past the closed record store and mostly empty restaurants. A bougie-looking bar with a fake rusted steel exterior—Amaretto, or something—promised, on a folding sign out front, a "New Wave Dance Party in Back!!!!!" with a two-dollar cover. The guy at the door was reading a book of poetry by an old college professor of mine, a circumstance about as likely as finding her in the flesh, a mother of three small children and dedicated Brooklynite, dancing in this Virginia bar on a Monday night.

"How are you liking that?" I said.

"What?" he said, withdrawing physically like he was afraid I was going to hit him. "Oh, the book. I think it's very lyrical, actually. Her use of poetic imagery is very impressive. It's unusual for contemporary poetry, in my opinion."

"You prefer the old stuff," Leslie said.

"It's all been downhill since Yeats," he said.

It rhymed with "Keats." I was pretty sure he was fucking with me. He took my two bucks—he let Leslie in for free—and stamped our hands.

"Wait, is anybody actually back there?" Leslie said.

He wiggled his fingers and put on a spooky inflection. "You'll just have to find out!"

We walked through the empty main bar, where a bartender was watching one of the *Alien* movies with subtitles on a small, silent TV, and through a red curtain to the back room, where the music was playing at a surprisingly loud volume, given that we couldn't hear it in the rest of the bar. Two very thin, very young-looking women were twisting desultorily to "Rock Lobster." A middle-aged Hispanic couple sat in a booth glaring unhappily at them. At the very back of the room, three large white men with elaborate facial hair stood in a semicircle drinking beer.

"Well, you can't knock 'Rock Lobster,'" I said.

We wandered over to the bar against the wall and I squinted at the scrawled drink lists full of word combinations that I didn't recognize.

"Well, I'm going to get whichever cocktail has honey in it," Leslie said.

The female bartender had a spiky haircut and intense silver eye makeup in honor of the New Wave dance party that was supposedly taking place.

"Does it usually get crazier?" Leslie said to her.

"They haven't done it for like a year," the bartender yelled with enthusiasm. "I think next time will be better. But hey, you're in on the ground floor."

"Safest place in a fire," Leslie said.

"That's funny!" the bartender yelled.

"What's a Wang Blossom?" I said.

"It's *so* good," the bartender said. "I'll make you one. If you don't love it, it's free."

"I'll have a . . . does that say 'Burning Fire Truck'?" Leslie said.

"It's supposed to be ironic," the bartender said.

Leslie ended up with something that tasted like honey *and* jalapeño. Why these details? The night felt forced, off-kilter. We were trying to have fun, fixating on what was available to us, but it was a stretch. In this desolate space—the song had segued, inevitably, into "Blue Monday"—we were just two more medium-young people paying too much for drinks, wishing, like the seven other people in the room, that there were more people like us present to . . . what? To prove that we'd made a valid choice in coming out, like moths justifying their attraction to light.

We shuffled around a little bit to signify dancing, but we couldn't keep it up, even when "We Got the Beat" came on. It required too much effort. We set our empty glasses on the bar and walked back out through the front, past the door guy, reimmersed in his poetry.

"Hey, listen to this," he said. "That loud hub of us, *meat* stub of us, *beating* us, senseless. Pretty badass."

"What do you think it means?" Leslie said.

"It's *poetry*," he said, exasperated with her ignorance.

In the car, we were quiet. I felt ashamed for taking a normal, not-great time as a rebuke to our ability to have a life that made sense.

"Fuck it," I said. "Maybe we *should* just go to Montana."

Leslie was quiet for a long moment.

"My sense of everything is so fucking gnarled and provincial," she said quietly. "I'm never going to see beyond myself."

"Well," I said. "I'm all for . . . enlightened self-interest?"

"That's not what that is," Leslie said. "I'm just selfish."

The right way to play this felt out of reach. I didn't think that she was any more selfish than most of the people I knew. But she was somewhat more successful at achieving results. I stole a glance over at her. She was sitting up very straight, with her hands folded in her lap, staring intently out the windshield. The epitome of formal grace, which was not called for in this situation.

"Come on," I said. "Impulsive cross-country killing spree with me? *Badlands*-style? With slightly less murder? Kenny won't let us stay much longer unless we start cutting the grass and shit. He told me I wasn't *appreciating his environment*."

She turned to me, and I could feel her eyes against my skull.

"I do love you, Pete," she said. "I wouldn't be bothering with any of this if I didn't."

She paused, maintained, at a glance, her Egyptian statuary pose.

"What are you the most worried about?" I said.

"Well, exactly," she said. "You don't know."

A couple of nights before Leslie and I were supposed to start driving west, I stayed up late with Kenny. Leslie was in the bedroom writing, emerging only to pad to the kitchen every couple of hours to grab a Corona and bring it back to her lair. (The household had collectively determined that Corona with lime, while not earning any style points, was scientifically proven to increase, and even improve, one's creative output.) After eleven o'clock, she stopped coming out so I assumed she'd either gotten into a groove or fallen asleep. Most nights like this I tried to keep up with her, or at least keep an eye on her, but since I was now promised a yawning future of some unknown duration in her company, it seemed wise to pace myself.

Kenny was unhappy that Molly had stopped responding to his text messages.

"I learned how to *text* for this girl," he said. "Now I'm hooked on that shit, and she's like, *nope*."

"That'll teach you to dally with twenty-first-century women," I said.

"It's not like I was heavily *invested* or anything, but it *is* pretty fuckin' rude. Least she can do is send over some more pussy pics, leave me with some memories."

"I'm sure she'll come back around," I said. Molly had told me she'd like to have sex with Kenny again, though she hoped they wouldn't have to exchange many more words, electronic or otherwise, in the process. They didn't share a workable *frame of reference*, Molly said, which was true enough, but what was that compared to wit and beauty? She could show him some Buster Keaton, he'd set her up playing the washboard . . . Of course, I'd slept with maybe one woman who wasn't a writer, and even she'd probably tossed off a couple of Briefly Noteds at some point.

"Have you talked to Julia?" Kenny said.

"Hmmm," I said.

"Well, she must've heard you were leaving, 'cause she sent me an email telling me to ask you if you wanted your stuff. Also whether you were going to keep paying your part of the rent. Also whether you'd decapitated yourself with my chain saw yet. Stuff like that."

"I guess I should come up with some answers," I said.

"I mean, I can hold on to some of your shit. I'll even move it for you if you toss me some cash. I'm sure you'll be back around before too long."

"Fuck off."

"For, like, a *visit*, man, Jesus. But while we're on the topic, do you *have* any, you know, *plans*?"

"We're subletting a place in Missoula from somebody Leslie sort of knows. We'll get shitty jobs or teach on the Internet or something. Etcetera, etcetera. What do you care?"

Kenny sucked in his breath.

"We have a lot of fun around here, kid," he said. That faux-TV voice was not his usual mode of irony. I sat up a little straighter. "But don't pull that rich-boy shit. Don't act like your life doesn't matter."

"Is this about Leslie?" I said.

"I don't think you've got any idea what you're *dealing* with, bud," he said. "You're a lot of things, but you're not some tough guy. Julia, you know, she was good for you. *She* was tough, but she wasn't *ruthless*."

"What is this based on?" I said.

"I *know* people, man. I've lived a minute. What's the line? She's the knife. You're the other thing."

"It's not my problem that you hate women," I said.

"Not yet," he said, and smiled like the devil. "Remember Julia? She's not gone anywhere."

I crawled down the hallway with the sun coming up. Leslie was sitting in the center of the bed leaning back against the wall, squinting into her open laptop. A frayed power cord hung in a low tightrope across the middle of the room.

"Whoa," she said absently. "Hello."

"Are you actually working?" I said.

"Nah," she said. Her eyes drifted across the screen like a cat's following a spot of light. Her fingers pounced on the keyboard.

"I mean, it's all work," she mumbled.

"What I was doing, too," I said.

"Sure, baby," she said. She typed something, stared at it. "Just make sure you're writing it down in your brain."

"It's all . . . somewhere," I said.

I looked up at her and she gave me a smile so tired it barely existed, just the slightest softening of her features in pity.

I woke up on the floor.

Last Part

L eslie walked as slowly as possible in the direction of the Rose. She was in it, she would say, more for the journey than the destination. Peter was already holding court, along with what had become, or in her case, been reinstated as, the usual Missoula crew. They were a minutely rotating variation on the people who would be with her until this phase of her life came to an end, forcibly or otherwise: teaching poets, singing bank tellers, drug addicts.

She crossed the Higgins Bridge, watching a kayaker do battle with a small man-made rapid in the late dusk. She thought he should stop with that before it was fully dark, though she couldn't quite articulate why. Boating at night, even with the streetlights set to come on at any minute, seemed unnecessarily sinister. There were plenty of daylight hours available for such activities, especially in late summer.

Now a car sped in her direction, the horn screaming in staccato bursts. She looked down to make sure she was on the sidewalk—where else would she be?—and watched as the car raced toward her. She heard yelling from the windows, male voices, something like "heyyoufuckingslutwe'reinacaaaaarr!" and then something wet hit her face, covering most of the right lens of her glasses. It was on her coat, too, and now her hands, sticky and yellow, and . . . mustard. Fucking mustard. What, sprayed from a bottle? A packet that had somehow disintegrated completely on impact? It was so outrageous, and so stupid, and there was no possible response to it. They were most likely drunk college students speeding toward a bad time at the police checkpoint down the road. But seriously. She was really quite covered in mustard.

"Did you see that?" she said to a couple walking toward her, a large bearded man in small shorts and a small woman wearing a cape.

"Nah," the guy said, though the panic in his eyes suggested he had, and didn't want to talk about it.

"They've been doing that," the woman said resignedly.

"Doing what?" Leslie said. "Who?"

The woman swept her arm around slowly. Everyone. Everything.

It was hard to clean her glasses off—the stuff just smeared. She was wearing the glasses only because she'd run out of contact lenses and the extras she had were still buried in a bag, presumably, or hadn't made the trip west somehow. The glasses were at least one prescription out-of-date, so everything had a slightly fuzzed-out, not-quite-real quality that she didn't mind. She felt in disguise with them on, playing at a style that was purely the result of necessity. They did, if she was inclined to make such things manifest, underline her recent bout of seriousness—she was a *writer*, okay, *Mom*? Peter said they made her look younger, like a kid dressing up, and at her advanced age, she wasn't going to argue with that. Maybe, if she never sorted out her contact situation, she'd never have to turn thirty. Maybe if she grew younger, Peter would somehow become an adult.

He'd left the house that day around noon, half an hour after he'd woken up, with his laptop and a couple of books on his back.

He was going to "work," i.e., wander from coffee shop to book-store to café until it was time to start drinking, which could be much earlier than five o'clock depending on whom he ran into out there. She didn't discourage him—let all impulses be allowed, even, nay, the smashing of a nursing baby's head, like Blake said—but she had her doubts about the efficacy of his methods. She'd been there herself, physically there, in the same damn places. And sure, now she was getting shit done, so maybe you had to kill a certain amount of time before your brain was ready for the real stuff. But it had nearly killed *her*, getting to this point where she could actually sustain creative thought for hours at a time. She would not object when Peter realized that his true calling was in PR, which he'd started doing part-time for the law school and was apparently, despite his bitching, quite good at.

Their third night in town, they'd sat, still somewhat stunned to be there, in collapsible camping chairs on the porch of their sublet. A group of people who looked to be in their sixties ambled past them, men and women in fleeces and polo shirts, drinking from Solo cups and plastic wineglasses.

"The ghosts of Christmas future!" a tall woman with close-cropped white hair yelled in Leslie and Peter's direction, raising her glass in a toast, and her friends cheered her.

"Jesus," Peter muttered.

"Don't worry, you won't live that long," Leslie said.

He turned to her, eyes suddenly wide with sincerity.

"You really think that?" he said.

"What?" she said. "No! I mean, I don't know. I guess the law of averages says you will, if you stop drinking so much."

"I'm not going to be stupid and reckless forever," Peter said. "Just until it stops being good material."

Leslie kept herself from the obvious rejoinder: When was it going to *start* being good material for you, exactly? She was drawing deep from her well of mistakes for her own work lately, focusing mainly on the things she'd broken. She saw no other option for the time being, though getting hold of decent subject matter would be useful eventually. If she calmed down and focused enough, she wanted to try journalism. It would be cool to get paid to be the straight man, for once, around people more deluded and worse off than she was.

It did seem possible lately, though, that there was a chance she was what she'd long imagined herself to be: one of the chosen few to whom the task of chronicling the inner life had been given. There were hours—single hours, sometimes just minutes—when her thoughts moved down into her hands and transformed into something different on the screen in front of her, an eloquent translation of what had been in her head into something smarter, more substantial. She was chasing that now. If she could get a few more of those hours, that might be enough.

There were external, if still muted, signals, too. A young acquiring editor had emailed her, wondering if she was working on a book; a college friend who worked for a literary agent asked if she was interested in sending in a sample. She was under no delusions that these things would lead to immediate glory, but she was pleased that the world was starting to vibrate lightly at her frequency. If it turned out she wasn't crazy to think she could be paid to write, it might turn out she wasn't crazy about all kinds of things. She hadn't shared news of these developments with Peter yet. It was bad, but she couldn't stand the thought of slowing her creative roll to manage his feelings. When—if—something important happened, she would tell him. Probably.

These thoughts occupied her as she approached the bar. She hoped her coat wasn't ruined. Under the streetlight at the corner of Higgins and Broadway, she saw more clearly how insane she would look, even in the neon shadows of the Rose, splattered all over in yellow. Having to *talk* about it would be the worst part—keep it light, but acknowledge the misogyny. Make it stand up as a wacky episode in the single-camera autobiographical sitcom of her life. She'd rather be stoned and writing. Barring that, she'd rather be the boy in the car, hollering into the dark at some tall bitch in a nice coat. His night's work had at least yielded, what, a *tangible outcome*: she'd been forced to think some more about what exactly she was going to do with herself.

Her friend Yvette was smoking in front of the bar, staring into her phone. Leslie felt the dull pressure of repetition, the familiarity of accumulated scenarios. She didn't want to have to drink enough to make the rest of the night interesting. Yvette spotted her and brightened.

"Hey, we were wondering if we'd see you tonight," she said.

"I'm here!" Leslie said. "But shit, I forgot my ID."

"Are you high?" Yvette said. "Nobody cares about that. And what's all over you?"

The exhaustion hit her again, a throbbing between the eyes, a desire to be struck mute. She exhaled slowly. She thought of plausible lies—she'd taken too much of something, her brother needed to be talked down from a crisis, whatever—but she knew it would get back to Peter, and anyway, she was supposedly an adult.

"I'd rather not get into it," she said. "Can you . . . can you just pretend you didn't see me?"

"Really?" Yvette said. "Are you okay?"

"Yeah," Leslie said. "Yes. I really am."

"Are you doing something sketchy? If so, can I join you?"

"I swear I'd invite you if I was."

Yvette gave her a thorough once-over, weighing, perhaps, the likelihood that Leslie's condiment situation was the result of an activity she should press harder to be included in.

"Okay, I haven't seen you," she said. "But you owe me. Preferably in the form of drugs. You owe me drugs."

"Absolutely," Leslie said. "Thank you."

"Nothing exciting's happening, anyway," Yvette said. "Peter's being funny, though. I like him."

"He's fine," Leslie said. "Give him a kiss for me. But not *from* me."

She took a different route back toward her house, cutting through the middle of town on Broadway, where college kids clustered in front of bars that she'd never been inside of. She was very glad she was no longer twenty years old. She thought about the book she wanted to read when she got home, a thin new novel about coming of age in Havana in the 1990s. It was a couple hundred pages long and she'd only just started. She might be able to get halfway through it before Peter came home. She had to finish the section of the story she was writing first, though. It wasn't *good*, but maybe it was getting better. She'd stick with it for a little while longer, at the very least, do some reading, then go back. If it still wasn't working when she went to bed, she could start something new in the morning.

Acknowledgments

I'm grateful to all of the friends, institutions, and industry professionals who helped shape this book, especially: Molly Atlas, Jeremy M. Davies, Joy Deng, Maris Dyer, Laird Gallagher, Lee Johnson, Laura Kolbe, Amanda Korman, Sara Martin, Lorin Stein, Nick Tenev, the Ucross Foundation, and the writing communities of Charlottesville and Missoula. I'm very grateful, too, to my parents and my sisters for their love and support.